By The Light Of The Harvest Moon

A Collection of Supernatural Short Stories

Kathryn Cockrill

To my parents and Barney, for always supporting me and to Tofu and Biscuit for the moral support and puppy cuddles

Foreword

Autumn, and the autumn equinox, is the perfect balance of light and dark before the dark overtakes the light. It is the time when, for a split second, the world stops completely before falling into darkness; the leaves fall, the moon has its time to shine and the landscape is painted in brilliant, burnished colour.

For me, Autumn has always been comforting, a time when I feel most at home, when the nights are long and the heat of summer disappears, replaced instead by the cold morning air. To me, the dark overtaking the light is a time of celebration, a time of strength and comfort and a time that is so intrinsically linked to femininity and our power. That's why, with these stories, I wanted to explore the idea of the darkness overtaking the light as comforting, as freedom or as the escape that each of the characters needed. Darkness is interpreted in many ways throughout each story, within the supernatural elements, the situations, the resolutions and the characters themselves and their strength.

I hope you find your strength and comfort between these pages and within these stories.

The air shifts in these mornings,

creeping around red-tinted maples,

painting the landscape as new,

blood singing under cable-knit sleeves,

rushing to sharp-bitten cheeks,

flushing in cherry-red stars at the ends of a smile.

We find ourselves drawn to winding roads

that cut through bark-worn limbs like gossamer ribbon,

shrouded on each side by a blanket of burgundy and rust

crunching under boots,

an autumn symphony falling into the crisp breath of fall.

We come alive, out of the hibernation of sweating summer months,

relishing the wind that sweeps through our lungs

brushing away the heavy, humid sediment that has coated our throat, our tongue,

weighed us down with August sun.

Now we begin again,

souls singing in a torrent of tireless magic

wound into the very fabric of us,

into the cinnamon and maple lingering in the morning dew,

into the cold snap frosting windows and noses,

into the fireside warmth and ember-dusted sunset,

we shake off the shells of seasons past

like leaves falling from heavy shoulders

and step into the embrace of autumn.

Contents

Disclaimer & Trigger Warnings

Each of the stories within this book has different trigger warnings. I have listed all the triggers found within each story at the start of each story so you are able to skip specific stories if need be.

Please also be aware that these stories are dark and discuss difficult situations and are therefore **not suitable for children**.

By The Light Of The Harvest Moon

Trigger Warnings

Abusive relationship (parental/authority figure), physical abuse and discussion of religion and oppression.

By The Light Of The Harvest Moon

Bells on the breeze

in the heart of the woods

beckoned deep into its embrace;

by the light of the Harvest Moon

our world dissolves into night.

We were taught fear,

taught to block our ears, our minds, our hearts

as freedom danced on the wind.

We were taught goodness was submission, subservience,

subjected to rules bound by walls

curtailed and corralled like cattle,

branded with sins we could commit,

backs heavy with the darkness that would encroach

if we weren't *good.*

But darkness danced in the air like raindrops-

-fanciful and beautiful-

-full of magic and music and revelry

and free from rules and fear and sin;

if this was *sin* it flew across my skin

and made me feel alive.

One bite was all it took and I was free,

crisp skin snapping under my teeth,

welcome for the first time,

one of the lucky few who found their freedom

under the light of the Harvest Moon.

Once a year, by the light of the Harvest Moon, the barrier between the world of the Fae and our world dissolved into the night; we heard the bells on the breeze and felt the spark in the air as it wrapped around our hands and beckoned us into the heart of the woods. We were told not to set foot in those woods while the Harvest Moon shone, the same stories spun through our dreams and nightmares as soon as we were able to walk; the Fae will trap us in their world, tempting us with decadent delights and magic and, once they have us bound, we'll be forced to repeat the same night over and over and over again. We were told they prey on the weak, on those with impure thoughts and that if we remain good and follow the rules, we will be saved from suffering at their hands. Parents used the threat of the Harvest Moon to curtail our disobedience, promising to throw anyone who misbehaved into the forest as the moon rose.

We were told they set up a lavish feast, with table upon table stretching as far as the eye could see, piled high with every food we could ever imagine, sweets and treats, freshly baked bread, juicy fruit, anything and everything our minds desired. But one bite and we would fall forever under their spell, the food rotting away to nothing but dust, the glistening tables crumbling to the forest floor as the wicked Fae cackled at our misfortune. We would be forced to dance, to skip over stones and twirl around tree trunks until our feet bruised and bled and even then, we would be made to continue.

We were told and told and told, these dangers drilled into us, any questions or curiosity shut down without reprieve. And, come the night of the Harvest Moon, we were dragged through the doors of the church and forced into the pews as the doors were locked behind us, thick, unrelenting chains swung through the handles, the key swinging around the neck of the priest. He regarded us with clouded eyes, mouth set in a thin line, skin sagging and sallow against the stark black and white of his collar as he stalked to the podium. There, he spat and raged against the Devil, declaring the Fae as nothing but his servants, doing his bidding to trap unwitting souls. His skin mottled red, fury shaking his jowls, as he told us of the sins we could commit, of magic and music and revelry and the darkness that would encroach upon our soul. And there we sat, until the Harvest Moon disappeared below the horizon, chased away by the sun, our eyes heavy and blinking against the light, forced awake all night lest we fell prey to the magic of the Fae in our dreams.

The town's obsession with the Fae didn't finish once the Harvest Moon set; no, it carried throughout the year, anything that the priest deemed devilish or magical regarded as more of the Fae's tricks. We were subjected to weekly lectures disguised as sermons, telling us how impure thoughts, alcohol, even music outside the carefully curated list were just another way for the Fae to take control of our minds. We were ferried from school to church to our houses where the doors were locked by parents entrenched in their own twisted belief, shuttering us away from the world. We were prisoners. I watched any light, any enthusiasm for life, die in the eyes of my friends, my peers as year after year passed by; they gave up, their own beliefs, their own desires swamped by the weight of the church, of the rights and the wrongs, the rules and the fear. The words spat at every sermon grabbed hold, burrowing into their brains, taking root in their lungs and spreading like poison through their blood. They regarded the woods with the same fear and animosity of our parents, fear becoming anger, chanting with the priest, condemning Fae none of us had ever seen.

I stayed silent, dragged along unwilling, sitting at the back of the church, even as my parents glared and poked and hissed, afraid I would attract the attention of the priest, afraid I would make a mockery of a society built on the unfounded belief of a prejudiced man. But even as his crazed eyes glared at me, ready to lash and wound, I stayed in my quiet rebellion. There was little else I could do, underage, under my parents' control, stuck in a town with no allies.

It infuriated him, being unable to control me. I could tell, as we drew closer to my eighteenth Harvest Moon, that even my small rebellion would not be allowed for much longer. More and more attention focused on me, everyone turning to watch as we walked into the church, the cold wood of the pew somehow burning hot under their scrutiny, my wrists bruised from the 'punishments' my parents and the priest had begun to inflict, the latest in a series of attempts to break any spirit I had left.

In the weeks before the Harvest Moon I was barely allowed outside of my room, the door locked, the windows shuttered and all my belongings removed. I watched as they took my books, condemning them as evil, and burned them in the garden. I watched as they ripped my clothes, allowing me only a few linen dresses, and snatched up the meagre makeup I had once been allowed. When I had no reaction, they become more incensed, the priest called over for frequent house visits as they cooked up test after test, convinced I was somehow enchanted by the Fae, simply because I wouldn't conform. I was shackled, the metal burning my wrists and ankles, forced to stand for hours on end in yet another attempt to break my quiet, my rebellion. I gave them no reaction.

Inside, I was frantically planning my escape, knowing that if I stayed much longer, I would be forced to submit or I would die. The hours stood in the corner of my room, legs and feet aching and bruised, left me with nothing to do but plan. And, as I planned and plotted, determined to end my own suffering, I began to hear bells.

Faint, at first, drifting through the air as I fought unconsciousness, dancing around my ears, so quiet I believed I had imagined them. After all, no one had ever heard bells outside of the night of the Harvest Moon. But, as the days and nights continued, blending into one hazy fever dream, the bells got louder, ringing in my ears, breaking through the heavy smog surrounding my room. I heard them, even as my parents and the priest came in to ask if I had repented and I waited, with bated breath, to see if they reacted, but they never did, staring at me, unflinching. And when I stayed quiet, the bells strengthening my spine, their lips curled, disgust running rampant in their eyes. They cursed at me, their hands flying, spittle hitting my cheek before they stormed out of the room, the slamming door ricocheting through the house. Each time, the bells rang louder, as if they were trying to block out the yelling and slamming.

Then, came the music, light tunes that danced in the air like raindrops, fanciful and beautiful, somehow bringing with it the smell of the woods and the feel of the breeze on my skin. I reveled in it, a sense of comfort I had never been afforded in this town overcoming my entire body, racing through my veins with a warmth that I craved.

Faerie music.

It didn't scare me, not the way it seemed to terrify the rest of the people in the town, the idea of the Fae. Instead, it made me feel alive, despite how battered and bruised my body felt. It flew across my skin and wound into my hair, braiding itself into my memory. If this was what they were all so afraid of feeling, I knew with certainty this wasn't the place for me. I had a growing suspicion that the place I needed to be was deep in the woods, far, far away from this place.

By the week of the Harvest Moon, I had a plan. I needed to get to the woods, to get to the veil between our world and the Fae's and I needed to cross it. But, in order to do that, to escape, I needed them to believe I had seen the error of my ways. I needed freedom from my shackles, freedom to move outside of this room, freedom to run.

So, as the sun dawned on the week of the Harvest Moon, I bowed my head as my parents and the priest entered, careful to keep my shoulders drawn and down, my eyes on the floor. I twisted my wrists against the metal to pinch the skin, tears springing to my lashes before dropping to the floor and I waited. For a few tense moments, no one moved and I braced myself for the next punishment. The priest's cold hand gripped my chin and it took everything in me not flinch, eyes burning a hole in the wood beneath my feet as he wrenched my face up.

"Look at me, girl," he spat, fingers clenching my jaw with so much force I was convinced he would shatter my teeth before I could so much as blink. I met his gaze for a second before forcing myself to look away, as if cowed. He made a smug sound before dropping my chin and turning to my parents. "Bring her to church. We will see how truly she has repented,"

With that, he turned and stalked out of the room, leaving an icy trail in his wake. My parents didn't speak to me, silently unchaining my hands and feet, the rush of air on my ankles and wrists painful after days of being shackled. The pain was welcome. It was a step towards freedom. I washed and changed quickly, after a prod from my mother; we wouldn't want anyone to see my bedraggled hair and dirty skin after days of abuse. The entire time, I kept my head down, refusing to put even a foot out of line; I only needed to keep this up for a few days, just long enough that they no longer had me on house arrest, chained like a dog. Just long enough to be rid of this place for good.

The heavy weight of the church settled on my shoulders as we entered, a hush falling over the chamber. I knew their eyes were on me, judging, zealous energy snapping through the air like lightning. I didn't resist as my parents walked me to the very front, sitting me down in the middle of the row; instead, I folded my hands in my lap, twisting the faded linen of my skirt between my fingers. The sleeves were long enough to cover the welts from the shackles, the redness rubbing against the fabric with each movement. I welcomed the sharp sting, reminding me why I needed to stay focused. Heavy footsteps traversed the wooden floor of the church, stopping in front of our pew. My mother's fingers pinched into my side, just below my rib, her signal to look up, pay attention. I raised my head to meet the priest's eyes, hating the way he smirked as I did, his lips curling over his yellowing teeth. Slowly, he leant forward, until his mouth was next to my ear, his clammy breath on my skin feeling like tar.

"I expect to see your enthusiasm, girl," he whispered, the promise of what would happen if I didn't hanging in the air between us.

Bells rang faintly in the air, followed by a tinkling tune, chasing away the uneasy feeling in my gut.

I can do this.

With a final look, the priest hurried back to the podium and began his sermon, eyes fixated on us, on me, for the entire time. I knew if I turned back, if I looked to the left, I would have the eyes of the entire congregation. But I stared forward, fixing a smile on my face, joining in with the chanting, the singing, forcing my mouth to say words that felt toxic on my tongue. I was the picture of subservience. When the sermon finally came to an end, and the rest of the congregation filtered out, I waited with my parents like a prisoner at the gallows. The priest slowly walked over, grabbing my face again, eyes searching for *something,* a flicker of disappointment appearing when he didn't find anything but passivity.

"Much better," he spat and I felt my parents slump either side of me. "I expect to see the same enthusiasm from now on," He stared at me, waiting for an answer so I nodded, not trusting myself to speak, mouth still tasting bitter. It was enough. He released my chin and we hurriedly walked out of the church. The second we stepped from underneath the arched doorway, the bells came back, louder than before, as if to erase the past hour. A small smile flitted across my face but I carefully schooled my expression as my parents glanced at me.

Four more days to go.

Each day passed uneventfully, the fervor with which the rest of the town, and my parents, watched me dying down until I went almost unnoticed. The priest continued to stare whenever he saw me, his gaze creeping across my skin, trying to burrow underneath but the bells brushed it away. Soon, although not soon enough, the day of the Harvest Moon dawned. I awoke with renewed enthusiasm, even as my parents flinched away from the world. I could feel it in the air, the magic, sparking and fluttering across my body in waves. I could feel the pull, the woods beckoning, crying out to me. I'd played this moment in my head every day since I decided to run and now it was here, I almost couldn't wait. The day seemed to drag by, the evening reluctantly falling away into night, the moon rising like a beacon. As we walked across to the church, the light from the moon bathed across my skin, warming me from the inside out. I fiddled with the beads wrapped around my hand, the final part of my plan, before letting them fall to the ground. We continued walking and, just as the church came into view, I forced a dramatic gasp. Both my parents whipped around to stare, eyebrows drawn together.

"My beads! They were in my pocket, but I can't find them. I must have dropped them back on the path. I'll go and search for them and meet you in there." My father opened his mouth to disagree but I had already prepared for that. "If I go in there without them, I won't be fully protected from the…" I lowered my voice to a whisper, "evil Fae magic,"

After another second of hesitation, he nodded and I turned and hurried back down the path. I'd dropped them far enough away that they wouldn't be able to see me from where we'd stopped, a fact I was relying heavily on. The darkness of the night would cover the rest of my movement, but I had minutes, if that, to get far enough that they couldn't drag me back. I had to time it just right, to reach the heart of the woods as the Harvest Moon reached its peak so the barrier would drop. There was always a chance they wouldn't follow me, that fear might stop them but I had a feeling their desire to control me, subdue me, outweighed the dangers they perceived in the wood.

As soon as I got round the bend in the path, I darted off to the right, towards the woods, the bells tinkling happily the closer I got. Mentally, I was counting down the seconds since I'd left my parents, wondering how long they would leave it until they admitted they'd let me go. I had no doubt they would bring the priest with them to catch me. The darkness continued to shroud me, shadows creeping round my shoulders and brushing my face and neck. Even in my hurried run, I could tell these weren't ordinary shadows, imbued with magic that covered my skin. As I entered the woods, I heard a shout behind me, followed by more yelling and adrenaline raced through my chest. I had enough time to get to the heart of the woods, but it would be tight. If the barrier wasn't obvious, if I hesitated, I'd be done for. My lungs burned as I pushed myself faster, the twangs of pain from my ankles and wrists radiating across my body with each thump of my feet. The trees around me began to change, from the thin, bare, wizened twigs to towering trees covered in leaves in golds and

13

ambers and rusts, like fire lining the way. The air was cold but no longer oppressive, easing each gasping breath I took. Then, without warning, the close-knit trees opened up into a massive clearing, a ring of fire in the heart of the woods.

I could hear the crashing of people behind me, the telltale cracking of twigs and leaves. They were maybe a minute or two at most. I stepped further into the heart of the woods, the bells I'd been hearing for days so loud and melodious that it almost drowned out the approaching crowd. As I approached the very centre, the light from the Harvest Moon shone through a gap in the trees, lighting the leaves in an inferno. As soon as it hit the ground, the air seemed to shimmer and ripple before falling in a wave, the clearing that, seconds ago had been completely empty suddenly full of life and magic. They had, it seemed, got some of it right when they tried to warn us against coming here; there were tables and tables of food, towers piled high with everything you could imagine, my mouth watering at the sight of them. At the centre, a cornucopia overflowed with fruits and vegetables, littered with autumn leaves and flowers. Decanters of liquid were dotted in between the food, sparkling in the moonlight, deep reds and ambers reflecting the leaves surrounding the clearing. But it wasn't the food that had me gasping, my heart pounding. Fae, hundreds of them, filled the clearing, eating, drinking, dancing and singing. They looked nothing like the villains we'd been brought up with; we were told they were tall and dark, with pointed teeth and ears, black eyes and claws.

Instead, I was greeted by hundreds of friendly, grinning faces, some with pointed teeth, some with pointed ears, some with eyes that shone like a cat's. Others had antlers or horns, their skin every colour you could think of, some even shining gold or silver, sparkling like diamonds. Each and every one of them was effortlessly beautiful, their clothes flowing like water across their bodies, dresses made of leaves dragging across the ground as they danced, barefoot, laughing. I wanted to stay there, watching their fun, a fun I had never seen before, forever.

A loud crashing snapped me out of my trance, the priest shattering the peaceful clearing, my parents and the rest of the townsfolk not far behind. They ground to a halt as they took in the scene, momentarily distracted from me. Fear shuttered across their faces, some of them stumbling back, clutching beads and muttering prayers. Even the priest was pale, his jaw clenched as he stared at the Fae. But I noted with interest, if I wasn't mistaken there was also longing in his eyes. I didn't have time to think about that though. The Fae had stopped their revelry at the crashing arrival of the townsfolk, staring at the group of them huddled by the edge of the clearing. I crept around the side as quietly as I could, not wanting to break whatever spell they had over the priest and the rest of the town. One or two of them glanced at me as I tiptoed over to one of the tables, eyeing the food. If the tales we had been told were right, one bite was all it took, and I'd be free. Fae shifted out of my way, letting me approach the cornucopia with gentle smiles. I reached out and grabbed a cherry red apple, the red the same colour as the autumn leaves, the smell enticing. I lifted it to my mouth but before I could take a bite, the Fae closest to me spoke.

"You understand that if you take a bite of that apple, you will be trapped in the Fae realm for eternity?" his voice was soft and lilting, with a hint of the bells I'd been hearing for weeks ringing as he spoke. I paused, but nothing about the Fae, about the scene in front of me, screamed danger and everything about going back with the townsfolk did.

"I do," I whispered, and he nodded, a smile flickering across his ethereal face, long midnight blue hair swinging as he gave a slight bow. I opened my mouth again to take a bite; as I did so the priest seemed to regain his senses, eyes raging and cheeks red.

"STOP! You're under their spell, under the Devil's spell! If you repent now, we will forgive you," he held out a hand and my parents stepped up beside him, their hands outstretched. "We will help you, girl, to see the error of your ways and seek forgiveness and freedom on the right path,"

Around me, some of the Fae muttered and grumbled, sparks forming on fingertips and teeth flashing, but my own rage was flashing inside my chest, bubbling to the surface.

"Forgiveness?" I spat across the clearing, my voice somehow loud enough to startle my parents, their hands dropping to their sides. "You call this forgiveness?" I wrenched my sleeves up to show the angry red welts, the skin raw from rubbing against the linen. The Fae around me hissed, the joyous atmosphere darkening, dangerous. But I knew it wasn't directed towards me. Their reaction buoyed my confidence. "You don't know the first thing about forgiveness, or about freedom! From what I've seen, the Fae are not the evil ones here," The priest reared back as though I'd slapped him

16

before taking two angry steps forward, shaking hand pointing at me.

"The Devil is already in you girl, you are wicked!" he screamed but any fear I'd felt before didn't reach me now.

"I am the only one of you who sees clearly. I would rather be wicked and free than trapped in that pitiful existence listening to your misguided, prejudiced bullshit," I smirked at him as I raised the apple to my mouth and took a bite, the crisp skin snapping under my teeth and the fresh juice dribbling down my chin. The second it hit my tongue, it was as though something snapped off of me, like a cloak falling from my shoulders, the weight of the town, of their existence tumbling away like leaves off of trees.

Free. I'm finally free.

The priest yelled and raged, gesturing, the townsfolk joining in the cry but it was like a distant buzz. The Fae who had spoken to me before, warned me, gave me another smile, this one softer.

"Welcome home," he whispered, "Would you like us to trap them here and force them into servitude for all eternity?" he gestured to the clamoring crowd but I was shaking my head before he'd finished.

"No. I don't want them anywhere near me ever again," I rubbed my wrists as I replied and his eyes darted down and back up, darkness flashing.

"Very well. We will seal this entrance to the Fae Realm altogether. No one will ever be able to enter through this clearing again," he muttered, and some nearby Fae nodded in agreement.

"What about next Harvest Moon?"

"We have other entrances to the Fae Realm, other places we can keep open so those few souls who search for their own freedom can find it here," Another smile before he turned back towards the edge of the clearing, striding forward, his height and presence enough to shut even the priest up. "Begone, foul humans, your evil is no longer welcome here," With a wave of his hand, the veil pulled back up, cutting the group off from view. The last remaining tension drained out of me, shoulders relaxing as the music started back up, the dancing following soon after. My feet began to move of their own accord but I knew this was no trick or spell; instead, joy bubbled up through my body as I spun across the bed of leaves, the light of the Harvest Moon shining down with all the warmth of the sun.

I'm finally free.

Afterword

The Harvest Moon is the full moon that falls nearest to the Autumn Equinox; it has long been considered an important time in the cycle of the year, holds spiritual significance and welcomes in the start of Autumn. Often associated with abundance and transformation or growth, it is also important in exploring our connection to the natural world.

The Fae or Fae Folk are often mentioned in folklore, particularly in relation to inhabiting a separate realm that is, in some way, connected to ours. Most of the time, Fae are portrayed as tricksters, tricking humans into eating their food and trapping them in the Fae Realm for all eternity. There are hundreds of different interpretations and tales of the Fae all through mythology.

In The

Tumbling

Moonlight

Trigger Warnings

Murder, gore/violence, mass death, mutilation

In The Tumbling Moonlight

Strands of silky red,

a ruby mane dripping warm

through the air,

entwining fingers like banners.

A woman sits atop a burgundy stallion

in the tumbling moonlight,

a promise, in soft waves,

of malicious intent.

Eyes shining with revenge painted red

the horse moves like magic,

scarlet and wine caught in its soft fur,

seeping through veins dappled with dove grey kisses,

surrounded by vile thoughts.

Green woodland coated

with slashed throats,

as sunlight filters through,

staining innocence

with a canopy of rage.

There is a legend we are told, as children, to keep us away from the woods.

We are told of creatures of blood and myth, with the teeth of a tiger and a horn made of bone.

We are told that they prey on those who ostracise, who condemn, who make a person feel helpless and alone.

We are told that they are tools of revenge for those who have none.

There is a legend we are told, a myth of blood and bone.

But we are also told it is only a myth.

The first person to go missing was a boy I knew, once upon a time. We all heard about it, the morning of the first Saturday of the year. I heard it when passing by a group of young girls, talking in whispers, looking over their shoulders every so often to make sure no one was near. They didn't see me until I had already heard their conversation and even though they immediately fell silent they could see from my face that their secret was out.

"Tucker's gone missing?" I kept my voice low, not wanting to alert anyone else in case this was just the make believe of little girls. One of them, the tallest, nodded at me, her brown eyes wide, bottom lip trembling.

"When?" They all glanced at each other, hesitation flitting across their faces. The tallest one spoke softly and quickly,

"Yesterday morning. That's what I heard my dad telling his friend at the police station." She drew back into the group when she finished talking, all of them reluctant to talk to me. I cringed internally, refusing to let my hands go to my face, a reflex from years of being teased. Instead, I nodded at them and turned to walk back in the direction I had come from. When I was deemed far enough away they started whispering again, although this time I didn't think it was about Tucker.

Maybe he's finally decided to do everyone a favour and skip town. Or maybe he got drunk and fell down a ditch. I can always hope.

Even in my head I could feel the venom behind my thoughts. I shook my head, trying to clear the haze and walked even faster back to my house.

I was walking through the forest, the moonlight too bright in my eyes, the shadows too dark. I heard Tuckers voice behind me, calling to me, telling me to come closer, that he wouldn't hurt me. Fear hit

24

the bottom of my stomach, dragging me down. I tried to run but I was tangled in dead leaves and branches. His voice got closer, louder, so close I could feel his breath on the back of my neck. I felt his arm reach out towards me but before it could make contact a piercing whinny echoed through the air and a flash of white darted across my vision. His voice stopped.

I woke up sweating, confusion making my sleepy haze feel heavier, foggier. I tried to tell myself it was just a dream, but something at the pit of my stomach clawed at me. The remnants of sleep crept back in, claiming possession of me, but the piercing whinny still reverberated in my ears.

They found his body the next day. This time it wasn't whispers that alerted me to it. It was the knock on my door, loud and persistent, that dragged me from a heavy sleep. I stumbled down to the front door, not turning on any of the lights even though it left my hallway shrouded in shadows. Cracking it open, my stomach dropped as I took in the uniformed man encroaching my porch. I opened the door fully, stepping back and drawing myself up to look him in the face.

"Officer." There was no question in my voice. I had gotten used to the visits, to the 'check ups', over the past few months.

"Lilli. Sorry to wake you." His voice was gruff, like normal, but there was an undercurrent of something else, something reluctant. It was enough to make the hairs on my arms stand up.

"Are you here to check up on me?" I raised an eyebrow at him and crossed my arms, keeping eye contact until he looked away. He seemed to gather himself before responding.

"In a way. Where were you Friday morning? Between 6am and 7am?" I raised the other eyebrow.

"I was here. In bed. But given that I live alone, and no one wants to associate with me, I can't prove that. You'll either have to take my word for it, or don't. Now why would you want to know Officer?" He shifted uncomfortably, taking out his notepad and flipping to a page covered in scribbles.

"Stanley Tucker's body was found this morning." My stomach rolled. "He disappeared around 5am Friday morning and the coroner has estimated he was killed between 6 and 7. Given your… history with the victim we have to consider you may have been involved." I rolled my eyes even though inside my heart was pounding. I could see what the police were thinking; I would be a pretty good scapegoat.

"You think I killed him?" My lip curled as I looked at the Officer, one hand still thumbing the corner of his notebook as he watched me. "Why would I even want to go near him after what he did to me? After he did all of this to me?!" My hand motioned to the left side of my face, the side the Officer had been avoiding looking at. I tried to keep the anger and the hurt out of my voice but it was there, at the edges, creeping into my words and clinging on with razor sharp claws.

"The victim's parents think you might want revenge." His voice lowered. I balled my hands into fists at my side. He noticed and leant back slightly, one hand moving to the stun gun resting on his hip.

"I didn't kill him. Of course, I wanted revenge. He made me feel safe, he told me he loved me and then he destroyed me. But I would have made him feel the same way he made me feel. I would have made sure he got stared at as he walked down the street, teased, whispered about, forced to be alone. I wouldn't have killed him. That would have been too merciful. So, if you would like to take me into the station then be my guest. But I had nothing to do with his death and I will not be your scapegoat. Not again." I held out my wrists, palms up and stared at him. He sighed, running one hand through his thinning hair and pocketed his notebook.

"Look Lilli, I'm not going to arrest you. We had to come and investigate because the victim's family would have lodged a complaint if we hadn't. They have too much standing in this town for me to ignore them, you know that. But I will tell them you had nothing to do with it. Given what his body looked like it was most likely an animal attack anyway. Just, maybe, try to stay out of sight for a bit? Until we close the investigation?" He trailed off at the end, looking me in the eyes again. I nodded and gave him a small smile. He nodded back and headed to his car waiting at the curb. As he drove off, I closed the door, hearing the lock engage with a small *click.* As soon as it was shut, I ran up to my room and began packing some things in a small backpack, enough to last me a night outside in case I had to run. Apart from that, there was nothing I could do but wait.

Another person went missing the next day, one of Tucker's friends. They found his body the day after. Then another. Another. By the end of two weeks they had seven bodies, all connected in some way to Tucker. All of them connected in some way to me. The bodies all looked like they had been torn apart by an animal, some kind of wolf or possibly a mountain lion. A couple of people threw around the idea of a serial killer. A couple of other people pointed to me. The whole town was in chaos by the time the seventh body was found, a mass hysteria. There was talk of hunting parties into the woods, although as far as I knew the only animals to live in those woods for the last hundred years had been a herd of wild horses, if they were even still there.

As the days drew on, I started going stir crazy, trapped in my house, especially when I couldn't help but feel that this whole thing was connected to me in some way. The night before the hunting party was due to leave my curiosity grew too much and I climbed out of my window, avoiding the cop car stationed outside of my house, with my backpack, and ventured into the woods.

The woods are not somewhere you go by yourself. They aren't pretty or calming. All the trees are malnourished, branches hanging limply from the trunk, leaves crumpled and decaying on the boggy floor. No one knew how the horses even survived in here, but there was no other wildlife. Barely any grass or foliage. Yet every so often someone would see a flash of white and hear a whinnying call echo through the trees. Under the light of the waning moon, I crunched through the undergrowth, listening for any other movement, any snap of a twig but the world around me had fallen silent. I knew it was a risk coming out here alone but I had no one to come with and no one would exactly notice if I went missing. As the night drew on and I trudged further and further into the woodland I began to wonder if maybe there was a serial killer after all. I had seen no evidence of any animals, let alone wolves or mountain lions. In fact, I had barely seen evidence of life.

It was only when the moon started to fade into the watercolour sky and the world around me turned a dusky grey that I heard movement behind me. A gentle rustling, barely audible but as I turned I knew I would come face to face with whatever had killed Tucker and his friends. I closed my eyes and spun round, opening them as I stopped. Whatever breath I had left seemed to fall out of me, a gasp of confusion as my eyes came to rest on, not a mountain lion or wolf, but a horse. It was gorgeous, standing a couple of feet taller than me, with brilliant fur, brighter than the white of the moon. Grey kisses dappled its neck that bent with a flowing curve, leading to a refined head. Giant black eyes stared at me, peering out from beneath a forelock of silky grey. Underneath that forelock I could see a bump, like bone, sticking out from his skull. It was small and twisted, coming to a point that peeked out from the silky strands, and covered in the same dappled fur that seemed to glint off the moonlight.

The protrusion reminded me of a unicorn horn, as did the horse, who seemed to float as it moved. Flaring nostrils moved closer to me, eyes bright and intelligent. As it reached me, it lifted its muzzle to my left eye, gently touching the scarring there, the slashes from a drunken knife and the betrayal from someone who had promised to protect me. I stayed still, holding my breath as it lipped at the worst scar, deep and forked that ran from my temple to my chin. Finally, it dipped its head, offering me its own dappled forehead. I reached out and stroked between its eyes, my hand just below the horn. On closer inspection it became clear that the horn was almost a disfigurement, jutting out from the bone, sheathed in fur. At the end there was dried blood, a dark burgundy colour in the early morning light. The horse seemed happy for me to stroke it, resting his muzzle against my stomach, completely calm.

Something about this horse pulled me in, like we shared a connection. Like he wanted to help me. My mind flashed back to the echoing whinny in my dream and the legend we'd been told as children, about creatures who protected those who had been wronged. We stayed like that for some time, neither of us wanting to move as the sun began to creep above the horizon. In my head I knew that meant it was around 5.30am. I had been in the woods all night and the only thing I had found was one of the elusive horses. More minutes ticked by, getting closer and closer to 6am. As the sun began to fully rise, its beams chasing away the grey shadows and coating everything in an icy light, the horse raised its head again, nostrils flaring once more as it scented the air. I almost didn't hear the footsteps behind me, so caught up in the creature in front of me. But the horse had. As my ears finally registered the crunch of dead leaves behind me, a voice cut through the silence.

"I knew it was you. You bitch." I spun around, eyes widening as I saw Tucker's mother storming through the woods towards me, closely followed by a group of people. She reached me, spots of colour on her cheeks, her eyes narrowed and flinty and grabbed my wrist, pulling me off balance. I stumbled away from the horse who was still watching the group of people, nostrils flared, sending puffs of smoke into the air. His neck was arched again, tightly coiled and I could see his muscles trembling, on the verge of movement. In the pit of my stomach I knew he wasn't happy. Tucker's mother dragged me towards the group of people, her fingers so tightly caught around my wrist that I had begun to lose feeling in my hand. She stopped in front of the group, holding me at arms-length.

"We've got her!" the group cheered, "I knew this little bitch was responsible for our poor children's deaths but the police wouldn't listen. Now we've caught her at the crime scene, they have no choice but to lock her up." Hatred began to rise in me again, against the people who had ostracised me, teased me, shunned me, all because of something one of their children had done. I had spent so long trying to keep myself out of their business, afraid that they would only find more reasons to hate me when they should have been the ones afraid of me. Of what their son had made of me. As I felt the emotions rise up, as the edges of my world tinged red, I heard hoofbeats behind me.

One moment I was held captive, the hand on my wrist pulling me forward and the next, all the pressure fell away. I heard screams from the people in front of me and looked down to see a hand around my wrist, no longer attached to its owner, dipping blood onto the decaying floor. Looking back up, I watched as Tucker's mother began to run, her arm erratically spurting ruby red blood. I saw a blur of white, heard a snap and she was on the floor, her head rolling a few metres forward, eyes wide and mouth open in a silent scream. Her body fell next to her, muscles twitching. The rest of the group had broken into a run, their feet stumbling through the undergrowth. More flashes of white flitted across my vision and one by one they fell also, limbs detached at various points. Their screams slowly died off and soon I was left once again with silence.

Reaching down, I detangled the hand from my wrist, letting it drop to the ground with a heavy thud. Turning, I locked eyes with the horse again. He stood, panting, steps behind Tucker's mothers body, his mouth and horn stained with her blood. He shook out his mane, still sparkling in the early morning sunlight and padded over to me, head lowered. I reached out a hand, trembling slightly from shock, and petted his forehead again. One by one more horses appeared, blood splattered across them, the same protrusion sticking out from their foreheads. My horse lifted his head as they appeared and threw it back in a whinny. Sunlight glinted across razor sharp teeth, curved and pointed, like that of a big cat. Looking around I saw that all of them had the same pointed, carnivore teeth. The whinny resonated through the trees, bouncing off of branches, singing in my ears.

I looked at the chaos around me, at the bodies, people I had known my whole life and I felt no sadness, no pain. They had caused me so much anguish, so much fear and now they were gone. With a smile I walked up to the horse, or I suppose, the unicorn, in front of me, and stroked along his side until I reached the base of his neck. Grabbing a fistful of mane, I swung myself up onto his back. As I landed, he wheeled around and took off at a gallop, heading deeper into the forest, the rest of the herd following behind. In the distance I heard sirens, but ahead of me I saw nothing but the chance to finally be free of the life I had been forced to live. I wound my hands deeper into his mane, leaning forward over his neck as the rising sun cut through the blackened trees and lit up the woodland like fire.

Afterword

The *Bo* or *poh* is a creature referenced in Chinese folklore that appeared similar to a unicorn but with tiger's teeth and claws that often devoured leopards and tigers. In some versions of mythology, the *Bo* would reward or protect those who are virtuous or innocent.

Season

Of The

Witch

Trigger Warnings

Burning at the stake/burning people, death of a loved one, assault

Season Of The Witch

"This is not a witch hunt."

You protest against pitchfork tongues
and barbed wire chokers
flush with your trembling pulse.

This is not a witch hunt
yet it feels like a trial:
subject to the whims of a council
who decide your fate.

This is NOT a witch hunt.

They claim, eyes full of flame -
flickering - ready to burn.
Unjust accusers leading the charge.

This is not a witch hunt?

You feel the fear against strong voices,

strong opinions,

strong women.

You question their defense,

their desire to pull you down,

to break you -

simply for being yourself.

You feel the charm, the pull,

magic wrapped in pretty words,

but you will not shy away.

There's magic wrapped in you.

This is a witch hunt.

But I will not be a victim.

I will not fall.

*T*he world was burning. No, I was burning. Flames were licking my ankles, their fiery tongues leaving a path of pain and blistered flesh. I could hear the screams of my sisters, their throats raw from the thick, acrid smoke but I could not see them, my world obscured by the tendrils of flame that leapt up to meet the sky. I struggled, twisting and turning, but the rope around my wrists and ankles did nothing but tighten, the coarse, frayed edges opening welts across my skin, droplets of my blood sizzling as it hit the flames.

I was burning.

The flames crawled up my legs, wrapping around my thighs, leaving nothing but excruciating torment in their wake; it was slow, the path of destruction, each inch of my skin painted black before the fire deigned to move on. As it built, growing taller under the night sky, so did the rage bubbling in my chest. I screamed, a battle cry that cut through the thick smog surrounding my body, forced forward by the same magic that had led me here. The faces of the onlookers startled as I met their gaze, the glee fading from their eyes as they were tried by the light of the moon and found guilty. I moved across each and every one of them, even as the fire climbed higher, wrapping around my torso like a corset, stray flames licking my throat. It scorched but I could not look away from them, all the people who condemned my sisters and I. The same people who came to us for a quick fix but turned against us to save their own skin.

I was burning. But so would they.

"By the light of the moon and the Goddess' grace, I set a curse upon this place,

As we burn by the heat of the flame, so shall all that share your names,

Take heed of this warning for it is too late, we await you and yours to meet your fate,

By the light of the moon and the Goddess' rage, I declare this curse shall never age!"

The last remaining embers of magic burst forth from my mouth as the final words of the curse settled on the ears of the gathered crowd, shooting into the air and falling like stars to the ground below. As they touched the grass, they burst into enchanted flame, brilliant white and blue, eating the ground in seconds. As the fire surrounding my body rose, so did my fire spread, the screams of the persecutors joining those of my sisters. Smiling, I tilted my head back and opened my mouth, adding my voice to the melody as the burning flames consumed me...

"Must be the season of the witch..." the music crooned into the car as I turned the corner onto Main Street, swinging into a parking space and quickly turning off the engine, cutting the melody short. I was amazed I'd got a space on Main Street; Oakbrook may have been small, but it was busy almost all year round but even more so in Fall and Winter. We were a quintessential New England town, complete with the red-bricked, charming Main Street, independent shops and so-perfect-it-seemed-fake landscape. Even now, as I clambered out of my car into the cool snap of Fall, the whole of the street looked as though it was about to appear in a Hallmark movie; Fall wreaths decorated every shop, maple leaves wound in vines around the lampposts and pumpkins dotted on every available surface. Somehow, even the air smelled of Fall, cinnamon and nutmeg dancing across the breeze, intertwined with the scent of warm apple cider and pumpkin pie. It was easy, standing here, to believe Oakbrook was perfect and, for a second, I let myself believe it. Then, the door of the store nearest to me swung up, bell tinkling, and the façade was broken as I met the gaze of one of the residents who immediately averted their gaze when they saw me.

I looked away, locking my car door before pressing my hands into the pockets of my Sherpa, the air cold enough that it brought me comfort.

Get in, get out.

I didn't come to Main Street if I could help it; hell, I didn't come to the town period if it could be avoided. Moving here when I was a teenager, it soon became apparent that we weren't welcome and my 'weirdness' only compounded the issue. Oakbrook loved outsiders if they were tourists, here to bring in some money and then leave, without trying to outstay their welcome. No one ever *moved* here though, the 'community' so close knit that it was near impossible to integrate. We'd tried, my mother and I, when we first arrived, talking to our neighbours, inviting them round for dinner, for BBQs, attending all the town meetings but we'd been met with suspicion and hostility at every turn. Even the kids, the ones I'd had to endure school with for four years after we moved, seemed to know the unspoken rules of the town and went out of their way to make sure I knew I wasn't welcome. I would never have anyone to work with in group projects, would find my lunch missing most days, only for it turn up at the end of the day, mashed and damaged in my locker. So, we'd started keeping to ourselves, our house isolated enough at the edge of town that we could avoid almost everyone if we wanted to. We only ordered groceries online, paying extra to get them delivered from the town over and I'd gone to school with my head down, leaving as soon as I could. I'd asked my mum why we stayed, why we even moved here in the first place and all she could ever say was,

"Darling, this is where we're *supposed* to be," She would never say anything more, except for one night, when she got drunk, and she told me in hushed tones that our family had lived here many, many years ago. When I asked her about it in the light of day, she denied everything and told me not to speak of it again. So, we continued, in misery but getting by. The worst was in the last year of high school, when 'not being welcome' suddenly became 'we want you to leave' almost overnight.

The first day of senior year, I'd come into school to find words were scrawled over my locker in bright red pen; *bitch, whore, witch.* Glances in the hallway became shoves, pushed into lockers and tripped round corners. It was as though a switch had flipped; more than once though, as I fell to the ground again, pushed by some unnamed student, it wasn't sneering or laughter I saw in their face.

It was fear.

Once I graduated, with bruises and more than one broken bone, I'd tried desperately to convince my mother we needed to leave, to go anywhere else but she had refused. Whenever I asked, her vision clouded, as though she wasn't even there anymore, and she told me we had to stay. Part of me wondered if I should leave, alone, even if it was just to the next town over but I could never bring myself to leave her. That's why I was here now, on Main Street, picking up her medication.

Another shop door opened and closed, the same bell tinkling through the crisp October air. Another set of eyes glared at me as I stood by my car, working up the courage to walk into the pharmacy. No one pushed me these days, instead giving me a wide berth on the street but I had this sinking feeling in my gut that told me this strange truce wouldn't last forever and soon we would be subjected to much more than a few glares once again. With a final deep breath, I pushed myself away from the car and down Main Street towards the pharmacy.

Luckily, there wasn't anyone else in there when I pushed the door open, even the bell sounded ominous when I did it, unlike the storybook melody that seemed to ring out for everyone else. The pharmacist behind the counter looked up with a smile as I entered, one that quickly dropped when he realised who it was. I didn't even need to ask anymore; immediately, he was plucking my order from a solitary box and placing it gingerly on the counter, like even touching something associated with us was taboo. Wordlessly, I threw the money down on the counter, the ritual familiar yet still grating and watched as he swept it into a bag before giving me a curt nod. The brown paper of the medication bag crinkled in my grip as I grabbed it and swept out the store before anyone else could come in and make this interaction even more awkward. The street outside was blissfully empty when I stepped back out, only inhabited by the various decorations strewn about, the Jack-O-Lantern's grinning cheerfully up at me as I walked past. Just before I reached my car, the warm light from a store window drew my eye and I slowed down, unable to tear my gaze away. The Oakbrook Diner was the most popular restaurant in town, that lethal combination of rustic charm and comfort food drawing tourists in like a honey trap and, even when the tourists left, it was still filled with a rotating cast of regulars, lounging in the booths for hours upon hours.

I'd tried going in once and had received such a cold welcome that I turned tail and ran, vowing I'd never go back in there. Still, as I stood outside in the cold October air, the smell of sweet pie wafting towards me, I *wanted* to go in. There were so many people in there, all of them chatting and laughing, their faces lit up and so *so* different from when they looked at me. One couple in a booth near the window were leaning close together, whispering, as the guy picked up a forkful of pie and offered it to the girl. She giggled, daintily taking it from the fork and I felt a pang deep in my chest.

It was so lonely here. I loved my mother, dearly, but besides her I was all alone. I wanted to sit in a booth with some friends, or a guy, and eat some of the pie that always smelled so delicious, and drink a hot chocolate overflowing with marshmallows and cinnamon and then, when we were done, we would stumble out into the crisp air, laughing, as the warm glow of the streetlights doused the walk home, no need to be afraid because we were in the picture-perfect town. Instead, the streetlights were harsh against my skin, the light grating, almost as if the very town itself didn't want me here. My gaze shifted to a family sat at one of the tables, the checkerboard tablecloth in its reds and whites screaming 'homecooked comfort'. The kids were playing across the table as their parents looked on, smiling indulgently, piles of food sat in between them, all of it looking so *good*.

I stared for just a second too long and the mother looked up, her gaze catching mine; her face instantly hardened as she muttered to her husband. In turn, everyone turned to look at me, eyes cold and mouths in thin lines. A chill that had nothing to do with the air outside rushed over me and I snapped out of my daze, hurrying back towards my car, risking a glance back at the diner when I was safely locked away. They had all turned back to their meals, the warmth of the diner and the surrounding Main Street back in full force even though the air and atmosphere surrounding me seemed to be nothing but cloying and somehow distant at the same time. I turned the engine over, the car humming to life under my hands and the radio flicked back on, the same song as earlier immediately starting up again.

Weird.

But, out of everything in my life that was weird, a song was the least of my worries. I sped away, already needing to be in the relative safety of our home and away from the Hallmark nightmare I seemed to be living in.

***

My body dragged me to sleep that night, my limbs leaden as I climbed into bed, the darkness rushing to claim me all at once, the duvet wrapped tightly around my chest like…

…arms grabbed me from behind, pinning my hands behind my back in the darkness. I struggled against them, trying to see who it was, to break their grip but they were unrelenting, fingers digging in so tight I knew there would be manacled bruises when… if… I got away.

"Let me go!" I yelled with as much courage as I could muster, even as my heart pounded in my ears. Their grip tightened further,

my hands started to go numb as they cut off blood circulation. I craned my head round, trying to see my assailant under the light of the moon but their face was hidden in shadow, the moonglow unable to break the thick darkness. I felt them lean in, their breath hot and damp on the nape of my neck drawing a shudder from me that seemed to travel across my entire body. They let out a low chuckle so close to my ear, the sound crawling up my spine, that I didn't even think, just reacted. I slammed my head back, feeling the satisfaction of connecting with bone, the crunch that I hoped was their nose and the muffled yell as they stumbled back, finally releasing their grip on my wrists.

I didn't stick around, wanting to escape far more than I wanted to see who it was this time. Luckily, he didn't follow me but I took the long route back, ducking into the woods surrounding the town and waiting for a while before exiting the other side and creeping back to my home.

It was getting worse, the violence, the attacks. I had a feeling that something big was just around the corner and I didn't know if I could survive it.

I woke the next day with phantom hands wrapped around my wrists, an ache deep in the bone that I couldn't seem to shake as I got ready and the vivid nightmare still playing over and over in my mind. It had looked just like Oakbrook but hundreds of years ago and every time I thought of it, this deeply unsettling feeling crawled across my skin. My mother murmured a few words over breakfast, her eyes unfocussed, as they often were these days, even with the medication. The doctors, one a few towns over because I didn't trust the one in this town, didn't know what was wrong so he'd prescribed a 'best guess' but it didn't seem to be working. As I was getting ready to go out for my morning run around the woods near our house, my mother suddenly reached out and grabbed my wrist, her grip surprisingly strong and her eyes now clear as day, staring into mine.

"It's your birthday tomorrow," I startled, shocked she'd remembered, or even knew what day of the week it was.

"Yep, the big 21. Yay for me," I couldn't even force excitement into my voice, the prospect of my birthday just like any other day in Oakbrook. I went to pull my hand back but my mother held fast, her nails digging into the skin on the underside of my wrist.

"This one is important," there was an undercurrent to her words I hadn't heard before, as if she was trying desperately to tell me something else.

"I know it is, Ma. I can drink now, which will be needed if we stay in this town for much longer," I tried for a joke but from the look on her face, I could tell it didn't land.

"I'm serious darling. This one is going to… change things. You'll need to be careful tomorrow, don't go into town."

"O-kay…" I tugged my hand back again and this time, she let my wrist go but her eyes continued burrowing into me. "I'll be careful Ma, I promise," She nodded after studying my face for a few more seconds before relaxing back into the chair and, as if I could see it happen, her eyes clouded back over again, her shoulders slumping and expression going slack. The same unsettling feeling from the dream clambered back up, gripping onto my shoulders but I shook it off, heading out the door for my run before anything else weird could happen.

The day passed quickly, as they often did when we didn't dare go near the centre of the town. Here, I could pretend everything was normal, that we lived in a normal town and had normal lives. But, as night began to fall and the moon revealed herself from behind the cover of the clouds, a heavy blanket seemed to settle over me, imbued with anticipation of… *something.* I struggled against sleep but it claimed me like a thief, stealing away the last hours of the day before I could even blink.

When I woke up on the morning of my birthday, everything seemed silent, still. The air didn't seem to exist, no breeze, no sounds of birds that I'd got so used to outside my bedroom window, no dogs barking in the distance. Instead, the world seemed hazy and stunned. I pushed back the covers, my skin burning hot despite the chill in the air and hurried to get dressed, a sinking feeling settling in my stomach as not even the stairs creaked on my way down to the kitchen. My mother was sat in her usual spot at the kitchen table but even she seemed to be on pause; I stilled at the entrance to the kitchen, watching her for a moment, waiting for some kind of movement but it wasn't until I entered the room that she looked up and, for a brief moment, a brilliant smile broke out across her face, the kind of smile I hadn't seen for years, not since before we'd moved to Oakbrook.

"Darling, Happy Birthday!" her eyes were unclouded and her voice was bright, a complete shock to my system. Cautiously, I took a seat at the table next to her and she handed me an envelope with my name scrawled across the front in her spiky handwriting. The paper felt almost soft under my fingertips, the envelope heavy.

"Thank you, Ma but what's this?" I asked, turning the envelope over in my hands. She laughed, another sound I hadn't heard in so long.

"Why, it's a birthday card of course! Go on, open it; I couldn't not get you something, it's your 21st after all!" At her urging, I slipped a finger under the tab and pulled it up, revealing a card covered in autumn leaves and gold writing.

Happy Birthday to my daughter

When I opened it, a wad of notes fell onto the table beneath me, more than I'd ever seen in my life.

"Ma? What is this?" I shuffled through the notes quickly, brain boggling at the sheer amount of cash in front of me.

"I thought you could go on a little birthday shopping trip to Pinebrook today, treat yourself to something nice for your big day!" She smiled again but this time it looked a little forced, the brightness not quite meeting her eyes. She must have seen the hesitation in my face because she continued, one hand reaching out to grasp mine. "Please, darling. I know you've endured a lot because we had to move here and this is my way of giving you back some of your freedom. I'll stay here because I'm not sure these old joints would be up for it but you can tell me all about your day when you're back," This time the smile was gentler as her calloused fingers stroked across the back of my hand. I could tell from the steel in her eyes that she wouldn't let this go and I admittedly wanted to go to Pinebrook. It was one town over, where Ma's doctors were, but we very rarely left Oakbrook so this would be a rare chance for me to have some actual freedom and, more importantly, no one looking at me like I was a freak on my birthday.

"Okay," I breathed, a small smile working its way onto my face to match hers, "I'll go. But I'm bringing you back some of that pie from the bakery near the doctors,"

"You do that darling," another smile, smaller this time and I could see the cloud hanging over her, about to smother her again. She winced, as if fighting it off, and squeezed my hand, "I love you darling… go and enjoy yourself!" With that, she shooed me out of the kitchen and upstairs before I watched her slump back into her seat.

I dressed quickly, calling a goodbye as I left, the excitement of spending a day outside of this town bubbling in my veins. Even my car seemed thrilled at the chance of a much-needed reprieve, starting up instantly and leaping forward onto the road leading out of Oakbrook. The weight that seemed to always follow me in Oakbrook lifted as we crossed the border, the open road weightless and almost endless. Pinebrook greeted me with all the warmth that a Hallmark movie *should* have and already, I didn't want to go back.

Hours later, laden down with a lot of bags, a birthday cake and the promised pie, I climbed back into my car to make the journey back to Oakbrook. The weightlessness I'd been feeling all day slowly changed, my body coming back down to the earth like a sandbag. But it wasn't until I crossed the border back into Oakbrook that it slammed down onto my shoulders in a painful wave, almost crushing me. I gasped for air, struggling to keep my car in the lane as this smog descended.

What is happening?!

I gritted my teeth and pushed forward but every mile seemed to force me further into my seat. It wasn't until I was round the corner from my house that I realised the heavy smog I thought was metaphorical was actually very much real. It filled the air, so thick I almost couldn't see the road in front of me and, as I turned the corner to our road, it permeated every inch of my vision. Only flickers of orange cut through, breaking up the dark grey, forcing it away from the windscreen. Blinking at the bright light after the thickness of the smog, it took me a second to realise that the orange was fire… and it was coming from our house.

"Ma!" the strangled yell tore from my throat before I could think, my hands acting on their own, slamming the car into park in the middle of the road and jumping out. The second I was on the street, the smoke seemed to part, brushing around me as I ran towards the blazing inferno that, just this morning, had been our house. "Ma!" I yelled again, ears straining to hear something, anything but only the crackling of the flames greeted me. They seemed to move out of my way as well, curving around my body strangely and, I realised, I couldn't feel the heat of them at all.

The front door to our house was ripped open, barely hanging on by the hinges but I paid it little mind as I stormed through, immediately racing to the kitchen. Ma wasn't at the table and for a second, a little piece of hope opened up inside my chest that maybe she'd got out, somehow. But a cough from the corner shattered that hope in seconds. Rounding the kitchen island, I froze, taking in my mother, slumped against the wall, coughing and beaten, burns blistering on her arms and legs.

"Dar-lin-" she broke off, coughing again as I sunk to my knees in front of her, trying desperately to ignore the blood beneath me that I knew was hers. She took another couple of heaving breaths before her eyes met mine, as clear as water now. "Darling," Her hand reached out, skin red and raw, and took mine; as it did, the flames that had been creeping along her body subsided, just out of reach.

"Ma…" tears slipped down my cheeks as I gripped her hand as tightly as I could, "Ma, what happened?" She didn't respond for a few moments, wavering, before she took a deep breath and began to speak, no longer coughing now the smoke had retreated.

"There's a lot I haven't told you darling. To be honest, I thought, well I prayed, that this was all some load of made-up rubbish. But the longer we were here… the more I felt it… I couldn't deny it any longer. I told you once before that our family came from this town, long ago. But it's much more complicated than that. We, our family that is, are witches."

"What?!" I interrupted but she fixed me with a no nonsense look, even with the bruising appearing around her eyes.

"Hundreds of years ago, we lived here, along with many others of our community, in harmony with the rest of the town. They asked us for help, of the magical kind, and they protected our secret from outsiders. For a while, it was peaceful. But then, the witch hunts began springing up across the country and, soon enough, someone, an outsider, visited our town, hunting witches. To begin with, the townspeople protected us, icing the outsider out but slowly, he began filling their minds with all of his beliefs, telling them we were evil, we couldn't be trusted, we would turn against them and kill them all. Despite years and years of harmony, they slowly began to believe him until the entire town turned against us, certain that we were evil creatures who would only cause them harm. They rounded us all up, your ancestors, the ancestors of many other witches who lived here and they… they burned us." Her voice took on a tone that wasn't my mothers, something other, and a breeze whipped around us, "They tied us to posts and gathered firewood at the bottom and they burned us alive as the town watched and cheered and chanted. Our sisters screamed and cried as they burned but we were angry too. We wanted revenge, revenge on the whole town. We cursed them, with our dying breaths, burned them where they stood and put a curse on their descendants, promising that they would meet the same fate." My mother's eyes turned milky white, like a film had been placed over them and her voice reverberated, suddenly two voices, then three, then four, all around us.

"But the curse didn't take so completely, not in the way we intended. It cast itself over this town and, when they came into contact with a witch, one of our descendants, they became almost possessed, casting out the witch, treating them like dirt, running them out of the town before revenge could be enacted, sometimes… killing them before they came of age if they tried too hard to be a part of the town… The curse draws us here, makes us want to stay here, to wait until we can enact revenge but it makes the townspeople want to get rid of us just as much." Ma blinked and the film retreated, just for a bit, "I'm sorry, darling,"

"That's why we're here," I whispered, "You had to come…"

"And I couldn't leave once we had. But I've never been powerful enough to enact revenge so the curse, it began eating me up from the inside out. It's slowly destroying my body, my mind and I can feel it all the time. I wanted to save you from it, my darling, you have to believe me but… I couldn't. I knew when you came of age, turned 21, the townspeople would strike, the curse forcing them to. So, I promised myself I would get you out, on your birthday, get you away from Oakbrook long enough for the curse to strike and then… then you could enact the revenge it's been seeking all these years."

"Ma…" the tears were streaming down my face now, as the fire continued to rage around us.

"Don't cry my darling, I wasn't long for this world anyway, not with the curse ripping me apart inside. But you, you can do this. You can beat it before it beats you…" she shifted, struggling against something I couldn't see, before her eyes clouded over again.

"They did this, the townspeople. They came here and they set your house aflame and they came in and beat your mother so she couldn't leave, couldn't move. They spilled her blood on the floor, and they laughed as they did it. But, the flames they set will not touch you; you can absorb the fire and make it your own and burn them from the inside out. We will get our revenge. We will take the pain they caused us, our sisters, our descendants and return it to them tenfold. *You* will set their world on fire…" At some point, the voices stopped coming from my mother's mouth and started in my head, reverberating around my skull, hundreds of them clamouring, screaming. My mother slumped, the milkiness leaving her eyes once more but now she seemed drained.

"Ma?" I whispered, already knowing what was coming next but not wanting to accept it. She gave me a watery smile, the hand I'd been grasping reaching up to touch my face, bloody fingertips cold on my cheek.

"I'm sorry, my darling, that I couldn't protect you. Please, give the curse what it wants. Get *rid of it.* Burn the town from the *inside* out. Then you'll be free, we'll all be free from this living nightmare. Just know, my sweet girl, that I love you… so much…" her hand dropped from my cheek, leaving lines of blood down my face like warpaint and her eyes dulled, the life leaving her like a flame being extinguished. Pain welled in my chest, my blood, my bones, beating through my body like a drum, ripping through everything else. Even the voices in my head, the witches, fell silent as grief tore through me like a wildfire, burning red, slowly morphing into rage.

The world around me flooded back in, the crackling of the flames, the smoke clouding the ceiling. It still avoided me, the fire cowering away from my touch but all I wanted, all I *needed* was to touch it, to burn, to somehow match this rage within me. I screamed, the sound guttural, cutting through the sound of the fire and, all of a sudden the flames seemed to suck in to me instead of cringing away, the bright orange and white rushing towards my body, hitting every single part of me. But I didn't feel the burn, didn't feel the heat, didn't feel anything but the rage, not just my own but the rage of a hundred witches, a thousand witches, all burned and buried, all aching for revenge.

When the fire stopped washing over me, when the room came back into focus, I could see the blackened skeleton of the house around me, the ash falling to the floor, the smoke painting the walls. But the fire was gone, resting in my chest instead, flickering and fueling me, propelling me forward, out of the door, down the street. I didn't go back to the car, taking off towards Main Street like the hounds of Hell were at my heels. The time it took to get there seemed to pass in the blink of an eye and the next thing I knew, I was storming towards the diner, flames thrumming below the surface of my skin, flickering at my fingertips.

The glass shattered as I threw the door open and everyone's heads snapped up towards me, the conversation falling silent. I saw the moment it happened, the curse taking over, saw the way they stiffened, saw how their faces tightened and, in any other moment, in any other timeline, I might have stopped for a second and seen them as victims of the curse. But in this moment, I wasn't just a witch seeking revenge. I was a daughter seeking justice for her mother.

One of the men nearest to me started to rise out of his seat but I held out a hand, flames jumping into my palm.

"I wouldn't suggest that if I were you," he froze as the flames licked higher. My voice reverberated throughout the diner, the power of all the witches before me carrying it through the air. "Who did it?" Silence greeted me, causing the flames to lash out as anger jumped in my veins. "Who. Did. It?" I ground out again, "Who out of you killed my mother?" the last bit came out as a wail, the sound so loud a few people covered their ears, wincing. Finally, a few more of the men stood up, faces hard as they looked at me.

"Evil witch," one of them muttered, spitting on the ground near me. I watched the spit land on the tiled floor for just a second before slowly raising my head back up to him. Fear flickered across his face as he took a step back.

"I am not the evil one here. I am not the one who killed an innocent woman. I am not the one who tormented a mother and daughter for YEARS. I am not the one whose ancestors burned hundreds of women simply for being born a witch, despite never posing any threat. I am not evil. But I will get rid of all traces of evil in this place, that I swear," my hand shot out, flames engulfing the man who had spoke, burning him up in seconds until all that was left was a pile of ash.

Burn them all, burn them all the witches chanted in my head.

I turned to the next man, arm raised, ready to attack when another voice sounded in my head, clear above the others.

Darling, killing them all won't get rid of the curse. You have to burn it out of them, from the inside out.

Even with the other witches screaming in my head, my mother's was loudest. A flicker of a memory, not mine, rushed in, filled with screams and burning and the original curse. As it faded out, more words filled my mind and my mouth moved of its own accord, the flame in my palm turning from red and orange to white and blue.

"By the light of the moon and the Goddess' grace, I break the curse upon this place,

As we burned by the heat of the flame, so shall all of the curse that remains,

Take heed of this warning before it is too late, lest you and yours should meet a different fate,

By the light of the moon and the Goddess' rage, I break this curse with Hellfire flames!"

The blue and white flames stormed out of me, engulfing the diner, spreading out onto the street. I knew, without seeing it, that it was covering the whole town. They didn't burn, not in the traditional sense, but each and every person in the diner writhed and twisted, screaming in pain as the Hellfire burned the curse from within them. I watched, with a flicker of a smile, as they experienced the same level of pain my ancestors had but knew that, unlike the witches hundreds of years ago, once the curse was burned out, the flames would recede, and they would be untouched. Slowly, as the flames worked across the town, the hundreds of voices disappeared from my head, the hum of their rage vanishing with them. The people in the diner relaxed as the Hellfire dissipated, all unconscious but no longer trapped in a twisted curse and only one voice was left in my head as the last of the town was cleansed.

Well done my darling girl, I'm so proud of you.

My mother's voice slowly drifted from my mind, and I tamped down the well of tears that threatened to overtake me. Now, for the first time in what felt like forever, I was free. I could go anywhere, do anything. I didn't know what that would be yet, but I knew the first thing I was going to do, once I'd laid my mother to rest, was leave this Hallmark-fuelled nightmare of a town and never come back. As I turned to the door, the sound system crackled back to life, shattering the eerie silence that had overtaken the diner and a familiar song blasted out.

"Must be the season of the witch…"

Afterword

Burning at the stake was a common punishment for anyone considered a witch, particularly in Europe in the early modern period; witch hunts have been recorded across hundreds of years, with huge numbers of women wrongly accused and burned at the stake, or later being subjected to hanging or drowning.

A Storm of

Sea-Salt

&

Vengeance

Trigger Warnings

Kidnapping, implication of sexual assault, death of a loved one, murder, domestic abuse, implication of mass death

A Storm Of Sea-Salt & Vengeance

They feared the sea, ruled as it was by the moon,

so they feared us too,

drenched in moonlight and sea-salt,

emerging from depths they could not fathom,

greeted with words of malice and magic,

battered by a storm of mistrust, uncertainty of the unknown.

We were wrenched from our skins, our armour,

shackled and bundled,

like nothing more than fabric,

trapped in a world that wasn't our own,

locked in cages made of compliance,

doused with bitterness.

They're still afraid,

clamouring, crashing, cringing,

caging us while our bones turn to driftwood,

forced subservience mistaken for control,

not willing, just afraid.

afraid to say no, afraid to run,

fear wielded like a sword against us.

But they forgot why they feared the sea,

complacent while they held us in wooden tombs,

forgetting that fire grew from embers

and fear could turn to rage like a wave,

no longer willing to be afraid of men

who claimed their 'power' from us.

We rose from the sea,

dripping with sea-salt and vengeance

pretty faces painted with vicious smiles,

shattering the silence imposed on us unwilling,

magic and malice clinging to our lips

and taking back our power under the light of the moon

until they once again feared the sea

and they once again feared us too.

In this town, there is a tradition. It's older than the grandparents and their grandparents before them, dating back to when they settled here, when the land was nothing but land and the sea frothed at its edges, writhing and ready to claim any unwilling victims that passed by. The sea, you see, was something their ancestors feared; they didn't understand its power or its creatures, didn't like the uncertainty lurking within the dark water and didn't trust the currents and waves, ruled as they were by the moon and the night.

So when the first woman emerged from the water, waves frothing at her hips and salt water clinging to her pale hair under the light of the moon, they feared her too. She moved as though the air was water, as though the waves still clung to skin, pushing her along the currents. She didn't speak, or not their language at least, eyes wide and dark as she looked over the townspeople, clustered together as though this single woman could take them all to the depths of the ocean. That first night, she said nothing, did nothing but observe and as the sunrise began to sparkle across the water, she turned and ran back to the welcoming waves, diving deep below the surface.

The townspeople waited for hours but she didn't resurface. They whispered, words of malice and magic, afraid more so now of the strange woman who didn't come back up for air. That night, when the moon rose from its slumber, the woman reappeared, gliding out of the water with a silvery sheen across her skin, standing just a bit further inland than she had the night before. This time, the townspeople moved closer, their uncertainty morphing into bravery in light of her silence.

They stretched hands out towards her, trying to touch, to grab but she danced away across the sand, footsteps as light as air until the water lapped at her ankles. The townspeople stopped, not daring to enter the vast expanse of water and, again, she watched them until the first hint of sunrise before diving back into the sea. Most of the town went back to their homes but one man stayed, watching the water for any signs of life.

As the sun rose, he caught a hint of her pale hair, swimming towards an enclosed bay to the east of the town. He hurried to catch up with her, arriving at the bay as she emerged from the water again, her skin glistening in the sunlight. Knowing he was intruding, he hid behind one of the jagged rocks at the edge of the bay, curious to see more. As he watched, she pulled something out from behind another rock; it appeared to shimmer in the light but was soft and pliant in her hands, a dark mottled grey. She glanced around, eyes wide, and he ducked behind the edge of his rock, waiting a few seconds before peering around again.

The woman clutched at the object in her hands, glancing towards the town one last time before swinging the object over her shoulders. It settled, like a cape, molding to her skin and began to expand, creeping down her spine and legs, across her arms, attaching itself to her body. Then, a blinding flash of light exploded out from where she stood. The man winced, covering his eyes until the light dimmed, blinking a few times to try and clear his eyesight. In the woman's place was a seal, resting on the sand, eyes as wide and as dark as the woman's. The man was confused, searching the rest of the bay for the woman, unable to find any trace of her.

The seal slipped into the water, dashing off into the deep, a few dapples of sun hitting the grey of its fur before it was enveloped by the crashing waves. The man stayed behind the rock, puzzled by what he had seen. He waited, as the sun crept overhead, blazing at midday and fading again in the afternoon. He waited, eyes fixed on the ocean until the sun dipped below the horizon. For a minute, nothing happened, and his shoulders slumped, but then the water parted and the seal appeared again, in the same spot it had disappeared from just hours before.

It looked around, deep brown eyes surveying the bay and, right before the man's eyes, the soft grey fur that covered its body began to peel away, leaving pale human skin underneath. Once it had almost all fallen away, the seal skin now on the sand, there was another flash of light and, once it had cleared, the woman stood there again, the remainder of the seal visible on her shoulders. She shrugged the seal skin off and bundled it up, stashing it behind the same rock, before diving back into the water towards the town. The man waited until she was out of sight before emerging from behind the rock, mind now set on uncovering the secret. He pulled the seal skin from under the rock, turning it over in his hands and marveling at how soft it felt, the skin covered in a fine fur that shimmered in the moonlight. He wanted it. He wanted *her*. And, he realised, she couldn't leave without her skin. He would not let her leave. *Ever*.

He waited, seal skin in hand, as the moon made its journey across the night sky, until the first ray of sun peeked from the furthest reaches of the ocean. Then, he hid behind his rock again, this time with her skin, as she emerged from the water.

She hurried over to her hiding place, hands reaching beneath the jagged surface of the rock for her skin. When she came up empty, he watched with glee as panic tore across her face, twisting into something inhuman. She scrabbled in the sand around the rock, desperately trying to find the very thing he held in his palm. When she finally stopped, defeat marring her beautiful expression, he stepped out from his vantage point, seal skin tucked carefully behind his back.

Her head snapped up, eyes wary as he approached, teeth slightly bared as though she meant to attack. When he reached her side, he held out one hand, keeping the other behind him still. She regarded him from where she sat on the sand, distrust written across her face. When she didn't take his hand, his expression twisted, sneering at the woman who looked at him so haughtily. Slowly, he pulled his other hand from behind his back, the skin glittering in the sunlight, drawing her eyes to it immediately. She leapt forwards, teeth bared in a snarl as a growl, the first sound she'd made on land, tore from her throat. He pulled the skin back, out of her reach, pushing her back with his free hand and smirking as she struggled.

When it became clear she would continue to fight, he pulled the knife from his boot and held it to the skin. She froze as the blade touched the skin, her face morphing from anger to fear. When he held out his hand again, she took it, sliding her delicate fingers into his palm, eyes fixed on his other hand that now held both the skin and the knife. He kept it just out of her reach, sure that the second she had an opening, she would lunge for it again.

Slowly, he walked her back to the town, yelling and shouting, rousing all the townspeople who gathered and followed as he walked through the houses. They clamoured around him, voices louder than the crashing of the waves but he would not answer them until every person had gathered. Then, he pulled the woman in front of him, dropping her hand and grabbing her hip instead, smiling triumphantly even has she cringed away from his touch, craning her head so she could still see her seal skin. The man told them how she would change from human to seal when she put on the skin, how she could not leave without her skin. He showed them how compliant she became once the knife touched the seal skin, letting him pull her around and show her off to the town. He called her a *selkie.* The townspeople, though shocked at first, soon realised what the man had uncovered; control. They were afraid of the sea, of its power and great mysteries but now, they had control over one of its creatures.

They would soon discover that they in fact, had control over all of it. For while they had dominion over the woman, they also had dominion over the water. The woman could bring the fish to the surface, could control the sea and its many creatures, keep them away from the town and its people or bring them to the water's edge to be slaughtered. The man, full of his own self-importance, announced himself as leader of the town and the woman as his bride. No one stopped him, no one spoke up for her and she could not speak for herself. For, he did not need her to be willing, he said, just to be afraid.

He gave her a human name, Rona, and dressed her in human clothes, covering her body from the eyes of the other men. He folded her skin into the smallest box he could, locking that box and hanging it from his belt, keeping her and her skin by his side. He taught her to speak their language, taught her all the tasks he felt a wife should know. Took her, unwilling, in his bed and told her to be quiet when she cried, saltwater staining her cheeks. Soon, her stomach swelled, and she gave birth to two children, a daughter and a son. The son did not survive, did not once cry. The daughter cried and cried, her cries echoing out over the ocean. And then, another woman, a selkie, appeared, drawn by the cries of the newborn. The townspeople captured her, located her skin and gave her to another man in the town. They learnt how to attract the selkie, to use the cries and the pain of their kin to tempt them from the water where they were immediately netted and captured.

The women became wives against their will, gave birth to both sons and daughters but only the daughters were born alive. The townspeople continued to exert their control over the sea, draining it of fish, of resources, selling to nearby towns and reaping the rewards. When the daughters of the selkie grew up, when they reached maturity, they would transform into seals for just one night before being forced to change back, their skins stolen from under them and locked away until a husband was found for them. The number of selkies drawn from the sea dwindled, though no one knew if it was because they had learnt to stay away or because there were no more left in the ocean. But, the townspeople did not worry. They had the daughters of the selkie, they had no need for more from the sea.

And so, in this town, a tradition was born. They did not take human brides, only selkies, the daughters of the town trapped before their birth. Men came from far and wide to marry into the town, the rumours reaching even the furthest shores.

***

It's that time again now; the newest daughters have come of age and transformed just once. *I* have transformed just once, the soft fur of my selkie skin settling across my bones for seconds before pain forced it away, ripped from my grasp like the crashing tide. We will all be married off, sold like cattle, chained to another horrid man, another power-hungry man, forced to kill our ancestral homes for the sake of their greed. I thought, naively, that maybe my father would be different, maybe he would spare me the life I watched my mother live. Instead, I watched as my father bundled my new skin into a tight ball before locking it away in a small box; he attached the box to his belt, the wood clanking against the other one on there, my mother's. He didn't spare me a glance as he looped the key back around his neck, tucking it beneath the collar of his shirt; my mother sat next to me on the worn velvet chaise, one arm around my shoulder, gripping into my arm with barely disguised tension. I snuck a glance at her face, her mouth drawn into a tight line as her brown eyes narrowed on her husband's pacing figure. She hated him, rightly so, with every fibre of her being.

I understood now.

Growing up, she told me stories of the world beneath the sea, a world neither of us had ever seen; the tales had passed down through the generations from the first selkie captured by this caustic town. My soul ached whenever she spoke of freedom we did not have, imagining diving beneath waves I had only watched from the window, travelling wherever the tide would take me. But, we could not. We were trapped, in this town and in these bodies; in the short time since I had transformed, an itch had settled under my skin, crawling through my veins, telling me that something was so very *wrong*. I was thankful, at least, that I had my mother with me; she had filled my life with laughter and magic, even as hers withered in a wooden tomb. Another spiral of hatred curled within the pit of my stomach as I looked away from my mother's frown and focused back on the man I called my father.

"It is done," he spoke at last, breaking the tension in the air. There was no hint of remorse in his eyes when he briefly met my gaze. "I will have you a husband by the end of the week." I bit my tongue, knowing all too well what would happen if I spoke my mind; I'd watched my mother suffer at my expense when I'd spoken out of turn before, her seal skin sliced, the same wounds appearing on her skin. When neither of us spoke, my father nodded once before turning away, slamming the door behind him as he left. Some of the tension leaked out of my mother's shoulders, her anger turning to sadness with a blink of her wide eyes. We looked at each other, matching tears welling in both our eyes.

"It hurts," was all I managed to get out.

I know my love, I know.

She spoke the words in my head, her lips still mashed together as if she didn't trust what would come out. The one thing the men of this town could not take from us was our ability to speak to each other without even opening our mouths. The one thing they never found out. Many simply believed their wives were mute and they preferred it that way, as did we. Being able to project our thoughts into each other's minds protected us and joined us all in a way they would never understand.

I leant my head on her shoulder, blinking as a couple of tears escaped and tracked their salty trails down my face. She rested one soft palm on the side of my head, stroking my hair and humming quietly. The men never got to hear our songs either. But my mother's sweet voice calmed my aching soul in a way nothing else could. The further away my father took my seal skin, the more the pain in my chest increased.

Is this how it will feel forever?

My mother's humming paused, her body tensing almost imperceptibly before she continued her song.

I hope it won't my darling, for you at least.

I let more tears fall, the reality of our situation, this never-ending pain, too much. To make matters worse, I had mere days before I was forced into the hands, and bed, of some greedy, horrible man. I had no misconceptions about that; he would view me as nothing but an object, power for his taking and nothing more. We understood our place in this world, but it didn't stop me from wishing it could be different.

The days slipped by, somehow moving all too fast and slower than molasses at the same time. Each day, I waited with bated breath for my father to announce he had found my husband and that I was to leave but each moonrise I was spared for another day. The pain of losing my seal skin didn't dull, throbbing in my chest with each crashing wave on the shore, but I started to become numb to it, staring out of the window to the water without really seeing it anymore. That evening, my father came back and I felt a weight settle over my shoulders; I could see it in my mother's face too. It was coming.

I sat at the table, hands twisting in my lap as he stomped across the room, heavy boots echoing on the wooden floor. My mother stood behind me, a hand on each shoulder, but neither of us spoke, not even in our minds. My father stopped, dragging a chair out from the table with a screech that made both of us flinch, and sat, staring at the table for what felt like an age. Finally, he took a deep breath and looked up to meet my gaze.

"You leave tonight. Pack your things and meet me back here before the sun sets," His deep, rumbling voice hit me like an undercurrent, the pain I'd numbed coming back full force. Even though I'd been prepared for it, even though I knew I was running on borrowed time, it still felt like the floor had been taken from under me. I could feel my mother's pain in my head but her face betrayed nothing, eyes fixed forwards, mouth in a straight line. Without another word, he left, the door slamming behind him echoing in the silence. I sat for a breath, trying to push down the tidal wave of emotion that was threatening to overtake me before I stood up and turned to my mother.

"Help me pack?" the question was barely more than a whisper, slipping out of my mouth before I could stop it. At the tentative question, my mother's resolve crumbled and she crumpled into me, arms wrapped tight around my midsection as she sobbed out loud. The second she broke, the tidal wave hit me too. We stayed like that for too long, the sun sinking lower towards the horizon before she pulled back, eyes still shining with tears.

We need to hurry.

She pulled me towards the small room we shared; she often chose to sleep in here with me than with her husband, unless he demanded it. With renewed energy, she threw my meagre belongings into a bag, pulling the strings tight and knotting them. The bags we used here were made from waterproof material and once you pulled the strings tight enough, water could not get in.

Go to your new husband, do as he says, no matter what it is but as soon as he is asleep, get out and meet me at the water's edge. I will be there until the moon sets. When he… goes to bed, he will take his belt off and your box will be loose. He is likely to be lax, forgetting to keep it out of your reach, since this will be your first night. Get the box and meet me. I will bring a key.

My brows pulled together as I stared at her, trying to comprehend what she was saying.

Mother… what are you talking about?

She smiled slightly, cupping my cheek in her hand.

You will not live my life, my darling. You will be free. I will make sure of it.

With that, she leant forwards and pressed a gentle kiss against my forehead. The door slammed open and she quickly leapt away, wiping away a stray tear from my cheek, her mask settling back into place. She passed the bag to me and I clutched it, my mind still turning in circles as I tried to work out what she was planning to do. My father never took his key off and he never let my mother close enough to it… except from when he forced her to warm his bed. I met my mother's eyes again, shaking my head but she simply smiled and tugged me out to the main room. My father grunted as we

71

came into view, nodding at the bag in my hand before motioning to the door.

"Come. He's waiting," My mother squeezed my hand as I walked forwards but she didn't follow.

I will see you tonight, my sweet daughter.

My father slammed the door behind us and gripped my upper arm, marching me forward. Our town, though profitable thanks to us selkies, was not big so I knew I had minutes at most before I met the man I would be forced to live with. Sure enough, what felt like only seconds later, my father dragged me to a stop in front of a door, shooting me a quick glance before knocking on the door. It swung open and I schooled my expression as I took in the man behind it. Easily twice my age, he smirked at me, eyes alight as they roved over my body. He looked much the same as all the men in this town, plain enough, and smelt slightly of alcohol and fish but his face was etched with cruelty. I had no doubt he wouldn't think twice about treating me as nothing but an object. My father silently handed over the box with my seal skin in and the man... my new husband whose name I didn't even know, grabbed it with eager hands, turning it over and shaking it. I felt sick as I watched. Then my father pulled out an identical key to the one around his neck, handing that over as well. My husba-captor slotted it into the lock; I was the only one who jumped as the lock clicked, the lid popping open. The second the sea salt air hit my seal skin, it was as though I could take a deep breath for the first time in a week. It was *so close.* My hand twitched at my side, aching to reach out and grab it from him but I knew I wouldn't make it more than two steps before they caught me. He regarded it for a few seconds, eyes flitting up to mine briefly, before snapping the lid shut and locking it again. The world seemed to press down on my shoulders again, my breathing shallow but I didn't let him see. I couldn't bear the idea of him knowing any more ways to torture me.

"All seems to be in order," his voice was jagged, bitter and putrid in the air. He grinned at my father, holding out a hand. "Pleasure doing business with you," My father, without even a glance in my direction, shook it decisively and turned away, leaving me on the doorstep. My husband stared at his retreating back for a few seconds before turning that evil smirk onto me. "Welcome home Cora," I jolted when he said my name but didn't respond. That would be too easy. When silence stretched for a few more seconds, he chuckled. "I see your father taught you well. You can call me Kerwin," I nodded once, earning another chuckle. He stepped back and motioned me into the house; my feet moved of their own accord as I resisted the urge to look back over my shoulder. The door shut with a quiet *chick.* I stood in a house that looked the same as my father's, all darkness and wood. Kerwin moved to the table, depositing my seal skin on the knotted wood, but kept the key around his neck. I kept my face carefully neutral, not wanting to draw any attention to his mistake. My mother had been right which made me wonder how she knew. Had she tried to escape my father? Had he done the same thing the first night?

I couldn't focus on that now. I had hours until the time my mother had set to meet. I needed to get through this as quickly as I could, no incidents, so I could leave. A brief thrill ran through me. *I might actually be able to get out of this.* I snapped back to reality when I felt his clammy hand on my face;

peering up, I met his cold eyes as he leered at me. This close, I could tell the smell of fish was on his breath; my stomach turned.

"You're a pretty thing," he murmured, stroking down my cheek, "I've been told you're obedient as well. Shall we see if that's true?" When I didn't respond, I was afforded another smile, accompanied by another hit of his fishy breath. "Good girl. Get on your knees." My blood ran cold and my eyes widened slightly; I watched his smirk grow. This was a test. And, if I wanted to make my escape, I had to play the perfect part.

Whatever it takes.

My mother's voice echoed in my head. I dropped the bag to the floor and sunk down, the wood hard under my knees.

You can do this. Just a few more hours and you can escape. Mother too.

I prayed that was true.

The moon glowed through the window, full and round, shedding light on the otherwise dark room. I welcomed it; I'd been frozen in time, waiting for *him* to fall asleep, waiting for his hands to no longer be on my body. Beside me, Kerwin snored, the sound grating in the silence. I risked sitting up, waiting for him to react. Nothing but another long snore. Quietly, I eased myself off of the bed, wincing at the fresh cuts on my back. Despite my best efforts, I hadn't been *obedient* enough for his liking. I picked my clothes up from where he'd thrown them, dressing as I hurried out of the bedroom. In the moonlit main room, I paused again. Another snore broke the silence and relief washed over me. Treading lightly, I hurried to the table, hands shaking as I snatched the box from where Kerwin had thrown it earlier. I didn't dare push my luck any further; I snuck to the door and eased it open, holding my breath as it creaked slightly, the sound all too loud in the silence. But the telltale snore came again, like clockwork. Slipping out into the night, I pulled the door shut behind me and glanced around. No one else was out here that I could see. I set off across the town, sticking to the shadows in case someone was still out or happened to look outside. I knew where my mother wanted us to meet; she'd taken me there as a child, to a small outcropping of rocks just past the view of the town houses where the frothing waves met the sharp edges of the stones and shattered. Away from the looming frames of the houses, my shoulders relaxed slightly, the openness and sea air bringing me comfort that no house ever could. But, seconds later, I could feel the tension seep back in; the rocks greeted me but my mother was nowhere to be found. I settled against one of the smoother edges, sinking down until I hit the sand; I couldn't go back to that house. Even if my mother didn't show, I had my seal skin. I had to run. I'd find somewhere to get it opened, another town, and then I'd disappear from this place. Free.

A shuffling sound made my head snap up, body tensing to run; as the figure stumbled into view, I relaxed.

"Mo-"

Shhh… not out loud my darling.

I clamped my lips shut and scrambled upwards, rushing forwards to meet her. She grabbed my shoulders and pushed me backwards, towards the rocks and away from the view of the town.

Mother? What's wrong?

As we stumbled backwards, the moonlight finally hit her face and I stifled a gasp. One side of her face was bruised, swelling, with blood dripping from her temple. Rage, pure and unchecked, slammed into me.

Did father do this?

She nodded weakly before tugging something from in her dress and pressing it into my palm, her hands cold against my skin. I looked down, eyes widening. The key.

You managed to get it? How?

My mother pressed a hand to the blood flowing from her forehead, hissing as she did.

I offered myself to him and during it, when he was distracted and vulnerable, I sliced the key from his neck and then stabbed him in the shoulder. He fought back and managed to get a few hits in but when I pressed the blade in further he blacked out from the pain and I got away.

I shuddered at the story, feeling her fear so close to the surface. With my free hand, I grasped hers.

Let's leave now. Where's your box?

Immediately, I knew something was wrong. She gave me a weak smile and squeezed my hand.

I couldn't get it and the key. He locked it away as usual and I didn't know how long I had before he came to; I had to get the key to you.

My heart stuttered in my chest. What was she saying?

I'll go back for it. I'm not leaving without you.

She was shaking her head before I'd finished, tears welling in her eyes.

You will be no match for your father and if he catches you, this was all for nothing. You must go by yourself, my sweet girl.

My eyes started misting over, tears rushing forward as I took in what she was saying.

I'm not leaving you, not with him. Not now…

We both knew how much she would suffer if she went back. But her face was set and her wide eyes were resigned.

I told you that I would not let you live my life. You have your freedom now and you need to use it. Find our kin and take them far away from this horrible place.

Mother…

The sobs built in my chest, even as I struggled to hold them in.

I love you, my sweet, sweet girl; go and live the life the rest of us could not.

I love you Mother-

"Bitch!" The word rang out from behind her, fuelled by anger and vengeance. Her eyes widened and she pushed me back quickly, motioning behind the rock I'd been leaning against.

Hide. And get your box open. You will need to leave quickly.

Heart thumping and tears still clinging to my lashes, I hurried behind the rock, fumbling with the key and the box. I turned the key and huffed a breath as it unlocked, the lid falling open willingly. I grabbed my seal skin, the softness thrumming through my veins and settling something in my soul.

Movement ahead distracted me; my father's figure stormed across the sand, one arm hanging limp by his side. The moonlight splintered across his face and I drew back, blood pounding in my ears. None of the impassive man I knew was left; his expression was twisted with rage, blood splattered on his skin. I realised, with a jolt, that it was my mother's blood, not his. She drew herself tall as he closed in but I could see the slight shake in her hands. As soon as he was within reaching distance, his hand shot out, closing around her neck and drawing her up, her feet dangling against the sand. She clawed at his wrist, gasping and twisting, trying to get air in.

"You bitch. How dare you try to leave me! Where would you have gone?! I still have this…" he motioned to his belt, where her box sat once more.

Maybe I can grab it…

No! Stay where you are!

My mother almost yelled in my head, panic tinging the edges. I clutched my seal skin closer, settling it over my shoulders. My heart was beating so loud I was sure he would be able to hear it but he was so focused on my mother that he never even glanced my way. After a few more seconds of watching her struggle, he sneered and threw her to the sand. Her body crumpled in on itself, gasping for air, one hand on her throat. I drew every breath with her, my gaze entirely focused on her, so close to my hiding place.

Click.

We both froze, turning to look at my father at the same time. White hot fear raced through my veins. My father levelled a gun at her head, eyes flat and mouth still drawn into a sneer.

No, no, no, no, no…

I couldn't move, even my breath frozen in my lungs. My mother took a deep breath, one hand still clutching at her throat. Then, she relaxed.

I love you, my darling daughter. Go, be free-

My throat choked up as her soft words filtered into my mind.

Bang!

The sound shattered the air, cracking across the sand. Then, there was a moment of complete silence where nothing dared to move. Finally, as if in slow motion, my mother's body fell backwards, hitting the sand, her hand tumbling out towards me. I could hear my heart in my ears, aware of the mounting panic in my chest, both hands pressed over my mouth so no sound came out. I wanted to move, to look away but I couldn't look at anything but the bright red blood trickling into the sand and her hand, stretched out towards me.

I kept waiting for her fingers to twitch, her eyes to blink, anything. But it never came. My father looked down at her body impassively for a few seconds, no hint of remorse in his eyes. Then he shoved the gun back into his trousers and turned to leave.

Run. Leave. You need to leave.

I shifted behind the rock, my seal skin scraping against the edge slightly, causing a fissure of pain to shoot down my leg, eliciting a hiss from between my lips. My father froze and slowly turned back around, eyes moving across the beach.

Shit. Move, goddamnit!

With one last glance at my mother's body on the sand, I took off running towards the ocean, my seal skintight around my shoulders. I could feel it melding with my skin as I ran.

"Cora!" my father's voice boomed across the beach, chasing after me like thunder. I heard the sound of metal against fabric and knew he had the gun back out but I was already at the water's edge, my feet splashing through the salty sea. Taking a breath, I dove beneath the surface, a bright light exploding out as I broke the waves. My seal skin melded completely, my body reshaping under the water, becoming smoother, faster. Instinct took over, driving me down, away from the air and the danger.

Only once I was sure I was out of reach of a gunshot did I stop, the full reality of what had just happened crashing down on me. I expected to feel more sadness, to feel a sob or tightness in my chest. I didn't expect the white-hot rage again, burning through my body like wildfire. As the last shards of the moon filtered through the water, the rage overtook and I *screamed.*

The water around me rippled, the sound carrying through the darkness. I screamed and I screamed, scaring away the fish that dared come close. I was sure it could be heard from the surface. Then, as quickly as it had overcome me, the rage petered out, leaving nothing but heavy silence.

I was alone.

You are not alone, child.

I whipped round, trying to figure out where the voice had come from.

Who's there?

Shapes moved all around me, flitting by in the darkness of the undersea. I couldn't tell how many there were, dozens if not more, all swimming in circles. One shape broke away from the group, heading straight for me. My body flexed, ready to dart away but, as my eyes adjusted to being underwater, I froze.

Another seal… no a selkie stared back at me, her eyes as wide and brown as my mother's had been. She stopped just a whisker away, gazing at me with a solemn expression.

We heard your scream, my child. We've been staying away from this place, we know what happens if we come on land here. We know what they do to our kind. But we heard your pain and we couldn't stay away. What happened?

I didn't want to relive it again. But, they needed to know.

My mother helped me escape… I was sold to my husband today but she told me to meet her at the water's edge and she would bring a key so I could get my seal skin back. She had to stab my father until he passed out to get away and give me the key… but she managed it. She just couldn't steal her own skin back as well. She told me to hide and my father found her. He… he shot her. He killed her. I ran before he could kill me too. But now she's gone and all of the women of my town are still up there and their husbands will hurt them so they don't try to escape as well. They'll torture them using their seal skins, make them bleed without touching them-

I broke off, not wanting to think about the fate I'd just surrendered them to. During my speech, the rest of the selkie had stopped swimming, moving around me in one protective circle. I could feel the rage begin to mount in them, seeping through the water like poison. The selkie in front of me was silent for a moment before her voice sounded in my head again.

This will not continue. They will shed no more of our blood. They will take no more of our daughters. For too long we have hid, afraid of the power of men who have nothing but fists and weapons. For too

81

long we have allowed fear to destroy the lives of our kin, our sisters, trapped in their second skins, raped and tortured. We are done allowing these men to take our power.

The other selkies hummed, pressing in around me, their anger simmering.

How do you suggest we take our power back?

She bared her teeth and it took me a second to realise she was grinning, though there was nothing happy about her smile.

Fair is fair, don't you think? Since they decided to take our skins, I would say it's only right that we take theirs...

***

The moon rose again and, for the first time in hundreds of years, women emerged from the sea. This time, nothing but sand and silence greeted them, the townspeople dulled from years of complacency, secure in their own feeble power. But these were not the same women who had graced their shores in the past. These women had honed their power and, most importantly, their rage. They shook off the salt water and sand, pale hair shimmering in the moonlight, eyes no longer wide with naivety but alive with fire forged through pain. These women could shatter eardrums with their screams and tear men limb from limb with their teeth. They advanced on the town, still slumbering, pausing only to look at a patch of burgundy sand that marred the otherwise perfect beach. The women continued to the town, splitting into smaller groups and approaching the darkened houses. They slipped in, silent as an undisturbed ocean, creeping through houses painted with the blood and pain of their kin. In pairs, they descended on the men, one holding a knife of sea glass to their throats, pressing just enough so that they awoke. The men, still believing they held the power, tried to shackle them with their voices alone, shouting and raging but the women did not move. They waited until the men quieted, fear blossoming in their eyes for the first time in many years. Then, they trapped them in their bodies, humming a low tune not meant for human ears, locking up their limbs and rendering them powerless. Each man succumbed, their eyes the only part of them that could show their pain and then, the women smiled as they carved the skin from their bones.

The last woman and her kin stood outside a non-descript house. They held hands as they slipped in, finding a man slumbering alone, gauze on his shoulder and no key around his neck. One of the women pressed her sea glass blade to his throat and he awoke, eyes widening as he tried to jump up but the woman pressed her blade in harder, blood welling along his neck. He froze, blinking a few times to try and see within the darkened room. Then, the humming began and he found himself unable to move, a prisoner in his own body. His heart pounded as another woman moved across the room. She stepped into the light, a vicious smile on her face, another sea glass blade in her palm. His eyes widened, recognition dawning but it was too late. She leaned in, her face inches from his and pressed her blade against the side of his face, ready to take his skin as he had taken hers.

"Hello, father…"

***

In this town, there is a tradition. The land is nothing but land and the sea froths at its edges, writhing and ready to claim any unwilling victims that pass by. The sea, you see, is something the humans fear; they don't understand its power or its creatures, don't like the uncertainty lurking within the dark water and don't trust the currents and waves, ruled as they are by the moon and the night. In this town, the selkie, women from the sea, hold dominion. They emerge from the water, waves frothing at their hips and saltwater clinging to their pale hair under the light of the moon. Smart humans fear them too. They move as though the air is water, as though waves still cling to their skin, pushing them along like currents. They don't speak, not the human tongue at least, eyes dark and dangerous, magic clinging to their lips; there are no townspeople anymore for a single woman stole their skins and took them all to the depths of the ocean...

Afterword

A selkie is a mythical creature often found in Celtic or Norse folklore who can shapeshift between a seal and a human; the legend goes that if someone stole a selkie's seal skin they could trick or coerce them into marrying them and the selkie could not return to the sea until they found their skin.

Down By The Loch

Trigger Warnings

Cheating, abusive relationship, implication of death

Down By The Loch

Oh, deep in the Highlands another woman does weep

down by the Loch as the light fades to sleep,

broken souls make for easy pickings

as misery drags them miles away.

A myth steeped in smoke and terror and brine,

dragged from the depths by the call of her pain,

eyes full of lies, teeth lined with blood,

one touch and you're stuck 'til your body gives up.

Oh, deep in the Highlands another woman does wail,

down in the waves, beneath the wind's gale,

trapped by the tar and wound through with kelp,

another victim to the charm of a monster's grin.

Oh, deep in the Highlands another woman falls silent,

water in her lungs, there was no use in trying,

tricked into the Loch, her watery grave

by the Kelpie who still lies there in wait.

*G*od, *I hate the rain.*

That was my only thought as the landscape rolled by, the Scottish mountains covered in a hazy mist of nothing but rain. It was, of course, always a risk coming to Scotland in Autumn, or most of the UK for that matter; but the rain seemed to cling to every nook and cranny here. I guess, at the very least, it matched my mood perfectly. Maybe I'd brought it up with me, banishing the sun with the sheer weight of my misery alone.

I watched a lone droplet track a trail down the train window, the bead of water cutting a path through the misted window before dropping off onto the tracks below, the same tracks we'd been on for hours now, the metal glistening through the onslaught of water. Every so often throughout the journey I'd looked up in time to see the towering mountains or vast lakes of the scenery and for a second, the awe they inspired chased away the cloud that had been hanging over me ever since…

Since *he* cheated on me, broke my heart and imploded my life all in one fell swoop. Sure, it wasn't like I *had* to leave but nothing in me wanted to stay. The pitying looks from my colleagues, my friends, the snide comments from my extended family when I didn't bring him with me to the big Sunday dinner, they all made me feel further and further outside of my own life. The real kicker though, had been when our mutual friends bailed on me to go out drinking with him and his new girlfriend, less than two weeks after we'd broken up, despite each and every one of them claiming they would be there for me and that he was a pig. Turns out all it took was the promise of some free drinks and the prospect of a night without me and my misery and they turned tail faster than the rain was falling outside. So, that night, as they got drunk and posted all over social media, arms slung around the guy I'd once thought I was going to marry and his new super skinny, super pretty girlfriend, I made a decision. I didn't want to stay here, in this same town, with the same people I'd gone to school with and saw at the pub every weekend. I didn't want to hold my breath whenever I went out in public, wondering if I was going to run into *him* and see that smirk, the one that would have had me giggling like a schoolgirl only weeks ago. I didn't want any part of it. Instead, I spent the evening looking up where I could go that was far enough away for me to be out of their reach but not so far that I needed a Visa.

Scotland seemed perfect. Remote, with no one I knew, a completely fresh start and, an added bonus, as far away from them as I could get without leaving the UK. The next day passed in a blur as I quit my job, packed up my life, avoiding my 'friends' and parents the best I could with vague responses and told my landlord I was moving out. I'd paid up until the end of the month and knew I wasn't getting that back so he didn't care. Then, all that had been left to do was lug my two suitcases across London to Kings Cross and hop on the next train to Scotland. I couldn't get all the way on one train, of course, but I wanted to be out of England before someone figured out I'd gone AWOL. Once I was in Edinburgh, after nearly five hours on this train, my plan was to stay the night and then make my way into the Cairngorms by the light of day. My late-night searching had already brought up a few potential places I could find a B&B until I got my life back under control.

"Ladies and gentlemen, we will shortly be arriving into Edinburgh. Please collect all your belongings before exiting the train," the tannoy blared overheard, startling me into action. I grabbed my handbag and then wrestled both my suitcases out of the luggage racks, muttering under my breath as both got stuck, causing a very dramatic exit from the carriage on my part. The train pulled up to the platform and nerves began to build in my gut; I'd never done anything like this, never been remotely impulsive in my life. But I was here now, and I had to make the best of it. A new start.

I let the rest of the passengers disembark first to save myself the embarrassment of fighting with my suitcases while other people waited to get off and then dragged them down the two steps off of the train, managing to swear only once when one of the wheels slipped down the gap between the train and the platform. Luckily, no one seemed to be paying me any attention, so I grabbed the unruly case and trundled over to some benches, looking for my next move. There was a smattering of hotels not far from the station exit so I figured I could head to the closest one, get a room and then head out to drown my sorrows at a pub. Enthusiasm renewed, I hurried out of the station, almost immediately coming to a halt as I took in the crowds, the cobblestone streets and the huge buildings. Despite living in a city for most of my life, it never felt or looked like this.

Someone bumped into my shoulder with a muttered apology, breaking me out of my trance. Finding a free room at a hotel proved to be a bit more difficult than I expected but finally, at the fifth hotel I went into, they had a room. I dumped all my worldly possessions in the small twin room before heading back out into the city, more than ready for some food and a drink or two while I processed the last twenty-four hours. Luckily, it seemed that pubs, much like hotels, were readily available and, this time, I didn't have to try five before I found a seat.

The inside of the pub felt much the same as any pub in England, with the glossy wood bar backed by rows of alcohol, the faded leather seats and booths and a healthy mix of locals and tourists scattered about the place. I grabbed a stool at the bar, the surface tacky under my hands and glanced around at the people closest to me. To my right sat a couple who were clearly tourists, pouring over a map as they sipped on pints; I gave them a quick smile when the woman met my eyes before turning away to look left. An old man was sat two stools down, nursing a drink, eyes tired beneath heavy set eyebrows and a flat cap, his mouth almost entirely covered by a thick beard. I looked away before he saw me staring, not at all sure he'd appreciate the intrusion. The bartender came over then and quickly took my order, directing me to a weathered bar menu when I asked about food. As I glanced down the menu, there was a sound to my left of someone clearing their throat. Looking up, I met the eyes of the old man next to me, now sparkling in amusement.

"If it's food yer after lass I'd recommend eatin' anywhere else," he chortled and I responded with a startled laugh, the rich and friendly timber of his voice surprising me. "But, if you've got yer heart set on eatin' 'ere, ye cannae go wrong with a bowl of chips," he lowered his voice to a whisper, "even here they cannae mess that up too much!" Another laugh bubbled up in my throat, the first in a few weeks and he grinned back at me.

"Chips it is then," the bartender nodded as I glanced at him before shooting the old man next to me a long-suffering glare which only served to make him chortle louder.

"Good choice lass," he grinned, "I'm Harry by the way," he held out a weathered hand. I jumped one stool across, dragging my drink along the sticky bar top before grabbing his offered hand.

"Bonnie," we shook hands for a second before he went back to nursing his drink, watching me from under his eyebrows.

"What brings yer to Edinburgh, Bonnie? Despite yer name, yer not Scottish are ye?" The smile slipped from my face as I was reminded exactly why I was here in rainy Edinburgh on a random Thursday afternoon.

"I had a bad breakup and decided I needed a fresh start," That was the quickest summary of the worst event of my life I'd managed so far. "Edinburgh is just a stopover for tonight before I head up to the Cairngorms," One thick eyebrow rose, disappearing beneath his flat cap.

"Ye must really want to get away if yer heading straight to the mountains lass. Anywhere in particular?" we were interrupted as the barman dropped a steaming bowl of chips in front of me, depositing a tub filled with single serve sauces and some cutlery next to it. I paused before answering Harry, grabbing a chip and popping it in my mouth, my stomach suddenly ravenous now there was hot food in front of me.

"I hadn't really decided yet, maybe Kingussie, maybe Aviemore. I just want to be away from the world, in the middle of the mountains, maybe near a loch or two so I can spend some time staring at the water while I try and figure out what to do next," the words all came out in a rush, more vulnerable than I'd intended but Harry just nodded thoughtfully.

"There's a lovely little B&B in Kingussie," he rattled off the name which I quickly jotted down in my phone, "and ye'll be in the middle of the mountains for sure there. Plus, there's Loch Gynack not far out, walking distance for ye, maybe not for me, that ye can visit for as much staring as ye want," I noted that down as well, grabbing another chip and dipping it in some ketchup as the conversation lulled slightly. When I glanced back up, Harry was staring at me, a slight frown on his face.

"What? Have I got ketchup around my mouth?" I asked, hurriedly grabbing a napkin and dabbing around my face.

"Nah, nothing like that lass. Just, be careful by yourself up in the Highlands, especially near the Lochs," I laughed and grabbed another chip.

"Why? Is Nessie going to get me?" I chuckled again but Harry didn't join in, still frowning.

"Not Nessie lass, there's things a darn sight more dangerous in those lochs… like the kelpies," he muttered.

"Kelpies? Like, underwater horses, right? I thought they were a fairytale," It was Harry's turn to scoff now, the sound blowing the hairs of his moustache.

"Kelpies are not just some myth made to scare children at night. They're very much real and very much a danger to anyone wandering around a loch too much."

"Okaaaay," I glanced to my right to see if I could move away a seat but it had been taken by another customer. As I was debating if I could leave my chips and some cash and make a run for it, Harry grabbed my hand.

"Listen lass, I know ye think I'm a crazy old man, and Lord knows I am, but I am telling ye the truth about this. Kelpies are much more than just underwater horses, they're ancient beings who draw people to them, looking for all the world to be just a horse but as soon as ye touch them, yer stuck. They'll drag you down to the bottom of the Loch and drown ye before eating ye piece by piece. They're not to be trifled with and they love to prey on women, especially if they're alone." A shiver went down my spine, the air in the room taking on a chill that hadn't come from the rain. "But," Harry interrupted, "If ye do find yerself face t' face with one, if ye can grab it's bridle, the thing on its face, ye can control it," He stared intently at me, searching my face for... something. I nodded, wanting to tug my hand away but for an old man he had a surprisingly strong grip. After a few more seconds, his expression relaxed and he let go of my hand, returning to his drink. The barman, who had been hovering nearby, quickly swooped in and extracted it from his grasp, earning a disgruntled grumble.

"I think you've had enough for tonight Harry. Can't have ya scaring away all the patrons with your stories!" he shot me a wink and some of the tension that had been sitting on my shoulders melted away. Harry grumbled something under his breath before easing off of the stool.

"I'm sorry if I scared ye lass but mark my words, you'll be glad I warned ye," with that, he ambled out of the pub and into the steady rain, droplets already hanging off his flat cap as he disappeared into the busy street. I quickly polished off the chips, the charm of the city and this pub having faded with the chill in the air. With a murmured thanks and some cash thrown on the counter, I hurried out of the pub just a few minutes later, bracing myself for the cold of the rain, and wandered back to the hotel, content to hole up in my room where no more strange old men could accost me with stories of mythical creatures.

The next day dawned just as grey and wet, the rain pattering on the window of my hotel room greeting me as I blearily opened my eyes. Exhaustion was clinging to my bones, the sheer amount of, well, *everything* that happened yesterday still weighing on my shoulders. But, I pulled myself up and got ready, a strange thrum of excitement curling in my stomach. Today was the start of a new life, in a new place, away from everything that was causing me pain.

Despite the sour note we'd left the conversation on, I'd checked out the B&B Harry had recommended in Kingussie and it looked adorable and they had availability for a few weeks so it was kind of perfect. Which meant I was hopping on a train straight to Kingussie; allegedly the B&B was only a five minute walk from the station and I figured even with two suitcases, I could manage to drag them across any kind of terrain for that long.

The station was bustling when I arrived, crowds of people hurrying to and fro, a mix of tourists and locals though the tourists were definitely the loudest, sticking out as they yelled to each other across the platform. I hoped I didn't stick out quite that much although with the two suitcases trailing behind me, I probably did. I wrangled them back onto the train without much issue as it was blissfully quiet and no one else had any luggage on the racks so I took advantage of the space and shoved my cases in the lowest rack instead of struggling to lift them as I'd done the day before. The train pulled away from the station quietly and smoothly, heading back out into the drizzly landscape that I was already becoming fond of.

After a couple of hours switching between staring out of the window and reading a book on my phone, the landscape suddenly changed to rugged highlands, the rain taking a short break as we approached the Cairngorms which gave me a front row seat to the stunning scenery. I spent the rest of the journey in awe of the outside, so different from the streets of London.

I definitely made the right decision.

We pulled into Kingussie less than an hour later, the small station nestled in between old grey brick buildings and open land. I could even see what looked to be the remains of a castle in the distance and another thrum of excitement shot through me at the thought of exploring everything I could. Suitcases in hand, I hopped off the train into the cold, slightly damp but fresh air, thankful the rain had decided to hold off for a little while longer and started the short walk to the B&B. Kingussie seemed to have one main street which most of the hotels and restaurants were on and the road the station was on joined that main street, meaning I got to see a lot of Kingussie on my walk. The B&B came into view, grey stone and big bay windows. Above the front door was a balcony bordered by an ornate white metal railing, making the whole place look like it should have been in a fairytale. The door swung open on my (very noisy) approach, the smiling faces of an older man and woman greeting me. I quickly explained that I'd come on a whim and was hoping they had a room available for the next little while which they assured me they did, ushering me through the door with muttered glances to the sky. Inside felt warm and comforting and every surface it seemed had been decorated for autumn, with pumpkin figurines and pinecones strewn across tartan runners and glossy wood furniture. A crackling fire from the dining room filled the entire place with the smell of wood and warmth, the flames drawing me in even as I continued to talk to the couple and the smell of food from the kitchen down the hall had my stomach gurgling, reminding me I hadn't eaten today.

The woman, upon hearing my stomach, told me to head up to my room and that she'd bring me up some food shortly after. I could feel the tears threatening to well up behind my eyes at their warm welcome, so I took the key and dashed upstairs before I broke down in tears in front of two people who had literally just met me and didn't quite need my whole life story yet. The room was just as comforting as the rest of the B&B, the bed huge and piled with tartan pillows, complete with its own selection of autumnal figurines. Despite the urge to have a nap, I couldn't wait to explore; it was an hour walk to the Loch Harry had mentioned but I still had plenty of daylight left to get there and back, with just enough time for some staring across the water. I wolfed down the delicious plate of food I found outside my room just a few minutes later before grabbing a small backpack, some water, my phone and a notebook and heading back out.

The rain had resumed but was more of a drizzle now, lightly misting my face as I set off, getting heavier as I left the village and started the trek up the single-track roads, skirting through a caravan park before heading into thick woodland. Just as I thought I would never see the end of the woodland, the trees parted, the slick path underfoot falling away to reveal the Loch, backed by a huge mountain and surrounded by green as far as I could see. Even the grey mist caused by the rain couldn't stop me from gasping as I took it in.

It felt magical.

I clumsily made my way down to the shore, slipping more than once on the wet, muddy path but thankfully I managed to keep myself upright each time. Picking my way across the vegetation, I stopped by a rock near the Loch's edge; it felt huge, especially with the towering mountain behind it and the water rippled and danced under the weight of the rain that was steadily getting heavier. I'd come all this way though, so I wasn't just turning tail and running at a bit of water; instead, I settled on the slick rock, the surface almost glassy, and faced out towards the Loch. Directly in my eyeline I could see a cluster of trees, a small island right in the middle of the Loch and wondered what it would be like to sit there and look out across the Loch back to shore. I snapped a few pictures on my phone but something in me just wanted to sit, the water calming in a way nothing else had been. My mind slipped, falling into the memories I'd been keeping at bay until now…

…*I opened the door to our flat, takeaway in hand, ready to tell Tom all about my horrible day at work but as I stepped through the door I was met with darkness. Strange, since Tom should have been back well before me. I'd told him I had to work late tonight, thanks to a last-minute task dropped on my desk this afternoon but I'd got through it in record time and even had chance to swing by our favourite Chinese place on the way back. I dropped the plastic bag* of food on the table so I could take my phone out of my pocket, just in case he'd let me know he was heading out but my notifications were empty.

Strange.

I shrugged, figuring I might as well get changed and then give him a call. I didn't need a light on to get to our bedroom, we'd been living here so long now it was practically ingrained in my brain. As I turned the corner to the hallway that led to the bedroom, I paused. Light was filtering into the hallway from under the bedroom door and now that I wasn't moving, I could hear faint sounds.

He must have gone to watch some TV in bed.

I crossed the hallway and pushed open the door, expecting to see Tom dozing in bed with his favourite TV show still playing in the background. Instead, I was greeted by long blonde hair and two very naked bodies that were definitely not dozing. My phone dropped to the floor, clattering on the wood and both of them froze. Tom's face slowly peeked out from behind the mass of blonde hair, all the blood leaving his cheeks when he saw me standing there.

"Bon-" The blood was pounding in my ears as I turned, picking up my discarded phone and ran back down the hallway. "Shit!" he muttered behind me before there was the sound of frantic scrabbling and footsteps pounding behind me. He grabbed me as I got to the door, tears already running down my cheeks, and pulled me round to look at him. "Bonnie, it's not what it looks like," he started lamely.

A laugh bubbled up in my throat even as I struggled to see through the tears. "It can't be anything other than what it looks like Tom. I'm not stupid. I'm also not blind. I could very much see that cow in our bed, naked, fucking my boyfriend!" I yelled, loud enough that he took a step back, hand dropping from my arm. Scoffing, I wrenched open the door, "Enjoy the rest of your booty call. There's *takeaway on the table, might as well eat it once you're done." With that, I stormed through the door and out into the rain...*

I couldn't tell if there was more rain or tears on my face. Somehow, it felt better that my misery was hidden by the rain, even if I was the only person here. I swiped at the tears before laughing at how futile it was as the rain just replaced them.

"Well, at least no one saw my minor breakdown," I said out loud, my words carrying across the Loch. The trees across from me rustled, something flitting between them but in the rain it was nearly impossible to see what it was. "Probably just a bird," I murmured to myself before movement to my right had my head snapping round. The whole Loch was covered in rippling water from the rain but a larger ripple was streaking towards me, much too big to be just rain. I stood up, backing away from the Loch as Harry's words from the night before came back to me like a gunshot.

"Kelpies are not just some myth made to scare children at night. They're very much real and very much a danger to anyone wandering around a loch too much."

The large ripple slowed, a few metres from the shore and I backed up even more, stumbling back towards the small track as the water suddenly went deathly still in that one spot.

Nope.

Without pausing to give it too much thought, I leapt back up onto the track, casting a couple of glances back over my shoulder as I hurried away from the Loch, the rain picking up even heavier now and plastering my hair to my head.

It was probably just a weird trick of the rain.

I tried to convince myself that Harry was full of shit, but I couldn't help but feel eyes on my back as I all but ran away, like something was staring me down. I didn't relax until I got back to Kingussie, rushing past reception up to my room and locking the door. Then, I took a deep breath and collapsed into the chair in the corner of the room. Now, back in the warmth of the B&B, the idea of something swimming across the Loch like that was preposterous, even though my skin still crawled. It took a couple of hours, a hot shower, some new clothes and a bit of time scrolling through TikTok before I felt ready to unlock my door and head back outside. Exploring was not on the cards this time, since night was falling and I had no desire to get lost in the Scottish Highlands today but a drink at the closest pub sounded like the perfect remedy for the creepy feeling sticking to my skin.

Luckily, it seemed like there wasn't short supply of pubs, even in the small town. There was one just a few doors down and the warm light coming from inside was a welcome sight. I pushed open the door and instantly the smell of home cooked food, cinnamon and woodsmoke hit me. A couple of the patrons glanced up but most of them ignored me, too focused on their own drinks or the heaping plates of food being brought out. Like the night before, I gravitated towards the bar, sinking into a stool and letting out a breath.

"What'll it be lass?" the barman appeared in front of me with an easy smile.

"Oh, whatever whisky you recommend," he nodded and winked, disappearing off down the end of the bar. As he placed the small glass half-filled with amber liquid in front of me, I heard the door open again and the room was suddenly flooded with the smell of seawater and something musty underneath. It disappeared after a few seconds as footsteps thudded across the floor, coming to a stop just behind me. I picked up my whisky and risked a glance over my shoulder only to be met by a wall of muscle. Leaning back, I looked up into a grinning face.

"Is this seat taken?" his voice was raspy, as if it hadn't been used in a while and something about it sent goosebumps across my skin.

"N-no, go ahead," I squeaked, turning back to my whisky as he sat down, the stool creaking underneath him. He muttered a drink to the barman but when I glanced to the left, he was staring right at me with intense focus. "Hi… can I help you?" my voice was barely above a whisper, but he heard it, smirking in response.

"Can't a man get a drink with a beautiful woman these days?" the rasp was growing on me, my cheeks flushing as he flashed me another smile. He was gorgeous, almost inhuman, with perfect features and long, dark wavy hair that seemed to glisten. Even his smile was perfect, brilliant white teeth gleaming in the low light of the pub.

"I'm sure you can find much more beautiful women in here," one eyebrow arched before he chuckled, grabbing the drink the barman set in front of him.

"I very much doubt that lass. No one in here holds a candle to you," he took a sip of his drink and I found myself transfixed as he swallowed, eyes flicking up to catch mine. They were so dark they looked almost black but that was probably down to the flickering, warm lighting surrounding us. It made for a cosy, moody atmosphere but wasn't great for actually being able to, you know, *see*. I shook my head instead of responding, choosing to take another sip of whisky, savouring the burn in my chest that followed. "I can tell you don't believe me and that is a crying shame," his voice, though still raspy, took on a musical lilt as he leant closer. "Why don't you believe me?" his eyes captured mine, holding my gaze with unwavering intensity.

"I-" *He's a complete stranger, don't scare him off with your tale of woe.* As if he heard my internal admonishing, he reached out and grabbed my hand, his palm warm against my skin and so soft it felt like water. Another smile, just slightly, and I felt my mouth open before my brain could even catch up. "My ex cheated on me with a much slimmer, much prettier woman… I- I caught them in bed together one evening and stormed out. The next day, he tried to get me to forgive him-

"You have to forgive me Bonnie, don't throw away all the years we've had together over something as small as this," Tom implored across the table. I'd chosen to meet him in a coffee shop, not wanting to go back to the flat after… everything.

"It's not small though is it, Tom? You cheated on me. In our flat, in our bed! I don't even know how long…" I broke off, a sob building in my throat, the pain from last night still a weeping wound. "How long, Tom?" He didn't respond for a few moments, staring down at his cup like it would answer for him. The sinking feeling in my stomach turned to lead. "How. Long."

"Six months," the answer rushed out of him but he wouldn't look up from the cup. The lead in my stomach turned to ash, the taste bitter in my mouth.

Six. Months.

"So you've been cheating on me for six months, presumably in our bed, and then I've been sleeping next to you after you fucked her, without even the faintest hint of an idea. God, do I need to get

tested?" Bile rose up in my throat, sitting at the back of my mouth as I willed him to look up, to just look at me.

"No. I… we never did anything without protection," He looked up then, like he expected a congratulations.

"Well, at least that's something. Yay for no STIs." My voice was acerbic; I wanted him to hurt, I wanted him to feel just an inkling of what I was feeling.

"Bon-Bon, we can get over this. It's over between me and her, I promise. You have to believe me, I never wanted to hurt you," I snorted at that. "I didn't, I mean it. Please, you have to forgive me," his eyes, eyes that I had previously stared into, imagining our wedding one day, seemed cold and flat now.

"I don't have to do anything. Just like you didn't have to cheat on me, but you did it anyway. I can't forgive you Tom, part of me wishes I could but I can't. I don't trust you anymore, I don't think I could even stand to sleep next to you. This, everything we had, it's over and that is your fault," I snapped, watching as his sadness slowly transitioned into anger and embarrassment. He sat back, arms crossed and regarded me with an expression I'd never seen before.

"It's not all my fault Bonnie. You're to blame as well; if you'd been there, if you'd been willing to go out with my friends more, if you'd put out more I wouldn't have looked elsewhere. We could have been happy but you let yourself go, you kept staying late at work and I had to find an outlet elsewhere." I stared at him incredulously as he rambled, the ash in my stomach igniting into red-hot rage.

"Are you serious? You're trying to blame me when you're the one who cheated? You son of a bitch. I never want to see you again; I'll be collecting my things this afternoon, don't be in the flat. Then I'll leave and I will not be coming back. So, lose my number and have *fun with your side piece. I hope she was worth it Tom because you definitely weren't." With that, I stood up and strode out of the café, refusing to give him the satisfaction of the last word. Once the rage died down, it was replaced by a bone deep misery that sunk its claws into my very soul, repeating every single one of his words on a loop...*

...I snapped back to reality as the smell of seaweed permeated the air around us; startled, I looked up to see if the door had opened somehow, but it was closed tight, not even a breeze sneaking through. I focused my attention back on the man in front of me and startled, just for a second, as his long wavy hair seemed to shift into hunks of seaweed. A second later, it was gone, his hair back to the long locks, his expression soft and his hand still on top of mine. It was only when he reached his free hand up and wiped my face that I realised I was crying again, tears silently rolling down my cheeks. He swept a few off and as his hand passed by his face, something like hunger seemed to light in his eyes before it was shuttered, replaced by the gentle look again.

How strong is that whisky?

I pushed the glass away from me, no longer sure I wanted to drink. We sat in silence for a few moments, until I stopped crying and then he spoke again.

"I'm sorry you went through that," his voice was even deeper than before, somewhat garbled, as though he was talking around something in his mouth. "That Tom guy sounds like a right idiot,"

"I can think of many stronger words, but yes, a right idiot is accurate," I snorted, slowly extracting my hand from underneath his palm. His mouth tightened for a second before relaxing back into that easy smirk.

"So now you're here?" his voice was back to normal, but I was starting to feel hazy, the world around me taking on a slight mist. I tried to blink it away a couple of times, but it wouldn't shift.

"Yeah… yeah, I decided I needed a fresh start, as far away from Tom as possible. So here I am," Subtly, I glanced at the other patrons, trying to figure out if anyone else was seeing the mist. "But I think all the travelling has got to me so I'm going to head back to my hotel," I smiled quickly before pushing myself off the stool, the world rushing up to meet me as I grabbed the bar top, trying to stay steady. The man watched me, still smiling, but didn't make any move to get up. "It was lovely to meet you," I murmured before stumbling to the door, the haziness descending even further over my vision. Outside the rain and wind had picked up, but I didn't even feel it, the water hitting my skin and running off. I turned towards the B&B, telling myself it was only a few steps away, but the path seemed to stretch further and further even as I walked and walked, never getting closer.

Frustrated, I stopped and spun around, but I ended up facing the same way again.

You've finally lost it.

My brain was foggy even as it made snarky comments, pressure building on the sides of my head. Gritting my teeth, I tried to walk again but I couldn't move forward. My feet seemed to have a mind of their own, taking me down the path I'd travelled earlier to get to the Loch. Distantly, I was aware that I shouldn't be going this way, shouldn't be leaving the town but I couldn't stop. The world seemed to pass in a blurry haze, the grey on the edges of my vision taking over until there was nothing but a pinpoint in front of me.

And then, as if by magic, I was back standing at the edge of the Loch, the path even more treacherous than earlier, swamped by the unrelenting rain. The Loch was pockmarked by the downpour, the trees in the centre almost invisible.

I was by the rock again. I didn't remember moving closer. But my fingers brushed the smooth surface, the cold rushing up my arm. I couldn't look away from the Loch so when the ripples started again, I saw it right away, even as it sped towards me. I couldn't move. A dark head broke the surface, covered by great chunks of seaweed and kelp, followed by a long face, flaring nostrils and brilliant white teeth. One hoof stepped onto the shore, followed by another until it was stood out of the water, rivulets of water casting tracks down it's pitch-black fur. Black eyes stared at me, drawing me in, even as my brain catalogued the *wrongness* of the rest of the creature. Rocks and moss seemed to cover its back, sharp and stained with something dark. More seaweed fell in a waterfall from its rump, dragging in the water and the scent of the water and seaweed saturated the air around me.

Kelpie.

As the thought entered my mind, it threw its head up into the air, letting out a guttural cry, nothing like the whinny of a horse. It chilled me to the core, sending my heart racing in my chest even as I stood rooted to the floor. Teeth flashed and I realised they weren't the blunt teeth of a horse either but fangs, sharp and glinting. When our eyes connected again, I felt its hunger, deep in my bones. And, just for a second, the image splintered, and a man was standing there, the man from the bar, his easy smile charming even as his eyes told a different story. Then the rain washed him away and I was faced with a monster.

Tricked by yet another man.

The same rage I'd felt with Tom started burning again in my stomach as the Kelpie stepped closer, each step feeling like thunder, until it was so close I could have reached out and touched it…

Touch it… touch it…

My arm stretched out and the image warped again. This time, the man from the bar reached his hand out to me, almost touching my palm. It would feel *so soft.* Lightning forked in the distance and the Kelpie stared at me again, lips pulled back in a nightmarish grin. This close, I could smell nothing but the water, the seaweed; it smelt *wrong.*

I snatched my hand back, clutching it to my chest and the Kelpie stomped one hoof on the sodden ground.

I don't want this. I don't want to be tricked, controlled, hurt by another man…

Harry's parting words came back to me in a rush. *"If ye do find yerself face t' face with one, if ye can grab it's bridle, the thing on its face, ye can control it,"*

Worth a try.

I took a closer look at the Kelpies face, trying to discern anything different in amongst the darkness. Lightning flashed again, lighting up the air around us for a split second and I saw it, nestled beneath the mane of seaweed, a rope twisted around the Kelpie's face, the ends trailing over its neck. I had one shot to do this.

Taking a deep breath, I forced my face to relax even as my anger brewed beneath the surface, all tension dropping and slowly reached out a hand.

I can't miss.

The Kelpie seemed to freeze, eyes tracking my hand with unrepressed hunger. If I missed, if I touched anything but the bridle, I knew it would be game over for me, dragged to the bottom of the Loch.

One more bolt of lightning and I'll have it.

As if the universe had finally heard my pleas, the sky lit up one more time and I darted my hand forward, grasping and almost sobbed when I felt the frayed rope beneath my hand. The Kelpie on the other hand let out an inhumane screech, rearing up, trying to shake my hand off but I held on fast, reaching for the reins with my other hand. As soon as I had both hands on the rope the Kelpie froze though his eyes still raged. I could feel its hunger as keenly as my own, could feel everything it was feeling, thinking. It was angry.

But so was I.

With a grace I didn't know I possessed, I swung myself onto its back, keeping one hand firmly on the reins. The rocks and moss melted away, not able to hurt me, just as the Kelpie seemingly couldn't. I tugged on one rein experimentally and the Kelpie moved with barely controlled power, wherever I asked. We were one now and I had a chance for justice. I didn't know if I would be tied to this Loch now, if I would live as the Kelpie did but I did know what I had to do next. I pulled out my phone and unblocked a once-familiar number, pulling up a new message and dropping a pin at my location.

Tom

I've had time to think about it and I forgive you. Come and meet me in Scotland, I have a surprise for you that you definitely won't want to miss x

I put my phone away and grinned at the thunderstorm rolling across the Loch, the Kelpie shifting restlessly beneath me.

I guess Harry was right after all. But this is exactly the kind of fresh start I need...

Afterword

A kelpie is a creature often found in Scottish and Irish folklore; it is often described as a shapeshifting spirit that is found in Lochs and normally appears as a horse-like creature however it can shapeshift into various forms, including a human. A common trait of the kelpie is that is has a sticky, tar-like coat and if you touch it, you'll become stuck and will then be dragged down to the bottom of the Loch by the kelpie to be eaten.

The

Descent

Into Hell

Trigger Warnings

Sexual harassment, sexual assault, suffocation, discussion of demons/Hell, burning people, murder, assault

The Descent Into Hell

"You were lucky,"

We're told by devils with fake concern

as if being plucked from the fire and thrown into the flame

was something we should be grateful for,

lucky that that was *all* that happened,

it could have been worse.

The descent into Hell is easy

when the world above is cursed,

when we're told not to tell

not to fight, not to cry,

told what to do with our bodies, our minds,

when we're told not to react -

that will just make it worse.

The descent into Hell starts young,

taught a secret code not given to them,

taught how to dress, how to smile, eyes down

so *we* don't cause issues for *them*

who can't take no for an answer,

who can't take rejection,

who can't take the inconceivable notion

that maybe we don't want anything to do with them.

They push us down this road paved with fire

and somehow expect us not to pick up our own flames,

our own Hellfire forged in the caustic belly of the beast,

they push us into a domain meant to break us, shake us to
nothing but objects

and act surprised when we take over the space they tried to
shackle us to,

when we find we've got fire in our veins too.

They cry wolf so we send in Hellhounds

and we burn their façade, so carefully constructed, to the
ground,

biting down until we taste blood,

until it finally feels like enough,

until we stand in the flames

but no longer get burned.

L *ucky.*

That's what they always called me, even when I was a toddler. I seemed to get out of any scrape, even when trouble followed me like a persistent wasp. My parents would often say they'd come out to the garden to find carnage around me, but I'd be sat there, playing without a care in the world and without a scratch on me. They told me that, once I was able to talk and they asked what happened, I would always say 'dog' and point at the air next to me. My parents would shake their heads and play along, asking me about my 'imaginary friend' who kept me out of trouble.

Of course, I have no recollection of that time of my life. My earliest memories are much later and as much as I wished for there to be a dog in my childhood, I never saw one, imaginary or otherwise. Instead, I was told repeatedly to stay out of trouble, my parents trying desperately to keep me inside, out of harm's way and I spent most of my childhood staring at the four walls of my bedroom, plied with all manner of toys, books, entertainment of any form as long as I didn't have to go outside. I fantasized of adventure, of worlds I had only read about, of magic and creatures beyond my wildest dreams. Sometimes, it seemed so real, as though they could come to life in my bedroom if I tried hard enough, vague shapes fluttering in front of my eyes before vanishing into nothing. Slowly the years slipped away, the world passing me by outside of my window; despite my parents insistence that if I stayed inside, nothing bad would happen, that didn't turn out to be true.

Trouble wormed its way in through the cracks and gaps in the walls, sneaking through slightly open windows on a breeze or skittering through the dark by the light of the moon. If it could break, it did break; things as simple as cooking pancakes turned into a kitchen fire that blackened the ceiling and destroyed half of the kitchen. The flames seemed to lick around me, not daring to touch a single hair on my arms but torching everything around me. My parents raced in at the blaring of the smoke alarm, eyes wide as they took in the devastation of the kitchen while I stood, spatula in hand, watching the flames grow taller. I saw it for the first time then, the flicker of fear in their eyes, as we hurried out of the house and into the street to wait for the fire department to arrive. It wasn't fear of the fire, it was fear of *me.* I assured them, repeatedly, that I hadn't even realised the fire had started as it seemed to catch in the few seconds that my back was turned and spread in a breath but I could tell they didn't fully believe me. I was banned from the kitchen after that, all of my meals delivered to my room, in another attempt to stop the chaos that followed me like a moth to a flame.

Of course, it didn't work.

Over the course of the next few years, the pipes burst and flooded the upstairs, windows shattered with startling frequency until they were boarded, my only link to the outside world cut off, furniture broke with just a look, splintering to the floor even if I was across the other side of the room. Every time, just before it happened, a tingle would flush across my skin and I knew that nothing was safe. Each time something happened, I saw the uncertainty take root in my parents' eyes, the nervous tension that gripped their frames whenever they entered my room, the hesitant way they hugged me. When I turned eighteen, the *incidents* as my mother called them, seemed to double down, barely a day passing where something didn't happen and I knew they were reaching a breaking point. So, in the dead of night, I packed a bag with the few things I owned that hadn't broken, spontaneously caught fire or disintegrated into thin air and snuck out of the house, leaving no trace I had been there except for a note on the kitchen table.

For the first time since I was a kid, I was outside, the fresh air filled with scents and sounds I'd been cut off from, even in the early hours of the morning. I had no plan, no idea how to survive outside and very little money but I couldn't turn back. I had no desire to see my parents begin to resent my very presence the next time something caught on fire. I had to figure it out and hope that my 'luck' held. I managed to walk until I found a bus station and got a ticket as far away as I could with the little money I had, to some small-town hours away. I tried to stay there for a while but all too soon the incidents started again, driving away any semblance of a new life I had begun to cobble together. I moved to a new town and tried again but it seemed like something out there had it in for me and all too soon I was running from another fire, another disaster, as fast as I could. After the fourth town, I figured out I had maybe two months before everything went to shit and so I began to move every two months, picking another town on the map, setting up camp for a few weeks and picking up some part time waitressing gig at whatever dingy diner would hire me under the table.

That was two and a half years ago.

My 21st was fast approaching as I arrived at the 15th town, another tiny slice of mediocrity in the middle of absolutely nowhere. I never picked a place in advance, just got off the bus when my gut told me to. The bus spluttered into the station, the engine all but giving out as we rolled to a stop. I was amazed it had even made it. I hurried off the bus before it did something like catching fire just out of my proximity and surveyed the newest stop on my self-imposed road trip, the battered welcome sign at the edge of the bus stop catching my attention.

Devil's Creek Welcomes You!

I snorted, shuffling my backpack higher onto my shoulder. No town welcomed me, not after things started going wrong. But maybe Devil's Creek would surprise me. There didn't seem to be much else on the outskirts, besides a few stragglers hovering near the bus station. A tiny sign just behind the welcome sign pointed in the direction of the main town but I couldn't see any semblance of civilization from here. It was just trees, their leaves starting to turn to Fall colours, threatening to fall at the slightest gust of air. It was going to be a long walk. I set off down the dusty path leading towards the main part of Devil's Creek wishing, not for the first time, that I had picked up a dog along my travels, so I'd at least have someone to keep me company in times like this. But I couldn't bring myself to potentially cause harm to a dog just because it was in proximity to me and whatever bad juju followed me everywhere. It didn't stop me from imagining though; I'd conjured up every breed I'd ever seen, sometimes wishing I had a small terrier to hop along by my heel and other times dreaming up a huge guard dog that came up to my hip. But most frequently, my brain presented me with a wolf-like guardian, with amber eyes and a thick coat I could bury my hands in during the winter. If I tried hard enough, I could almost see him trotting alongside me as I hurried down the dusty track, Devil's Creek slowly coming into view over the horizon.

The beep of a car horn shattered my illusion, startling me back to the present just in time to see a truck career past, two college guys leaning out of the windows, yelling and hollering. I ignored them, a skill I'd honed over the years; I'd very quickly learnt that if I engaged, it would only bring more trouble but if I ignored them, they lost interest and carried on. The truck seemed to slow for a split second and my chest tightened, wondering if I was going to have to leave Devil's Creek before I'd even really got there, but then it sped off again, the tires kicking up so much dust I was pretty sure I was coated in a layer of grime.

"Idiots," I muttered, wiping a hand over my face to try and remove some of the dust before I tracked down the nearest hole in the wall diner. Sure enough, as the first buildings of Devil's Creek appeared in front of me, one of the first up was a run-down diner with three cars sparsely decorating the parking lot and a flickering streetlight desperately trying to provide some kind of light above the doorway. I shouldered the door open, glancing quickly at the name, *Devil's Creek Diner*, before continuing inside. It smelt the same as every diner I'd come across, the bacon grease and coffee scent so familiar it made me smile. One very bored waitress looked up as I walked in, her eyes quickly flicking across my outfit and, no doubt, the dust I was covered in, before she forced a weak smile.

"Welcome to the Devil's Creek Diner, table for one?" her voice was like sandpaper, scratching up her throat as the smile wavered. I flashed her a quick smile in response.

"Actually, I'm here for a job. I've got two and a half years' experience as a waitress, and I'll only be here for a couple of months so I don't even need to be on the books…" I trailed off as she held up a hand before yelling over her shoulder into the kitchen. The doors swung open, and a huge guy lumbered out, wiping his hands on a stained apron as he stopped next to the waitress.

"What's up?" he grunted, giving me a critical once over before focusing his attention on the waitress again.

"She wants a job, under the table. I figured she'd better talk to you," she muttered, "If she wants some of my shifts, she can have 'em. Lord knows I don't want to spend every day staring at empty tables," The man grunted again and the waitress nodded at me once before heading through the doors he'd come out of.

"Ya want a job?" I resisted the urge to shrink back under his scrutiny and nodded.

"Yes, just for a couple of months while I'm in town. I don't need to be on the books, don't need any kind of benefits, just a job and maybe a place to stay if you have any back rooms that you don't use." He was silent for what felt like minutes but was probably only seconds before grunting again and spinning on his heel, striding back towards the kitchen. I stared at his retreating back, trying to figure out what had just happened, when he glanced over his shoulder.

"Ya comin' or not?" I skirted past the hostess stand and across the dated linoleum floor, following him as he shouldered back through the swinging doors. The waitress looked up as we came through from her perch on a couple of upturned milk crates and gave me a nod before looking back at her phone. Eventually, the man stopped in front of a door, turning his huge form back to look at me. "If you're willin' to pick up the shifts no one else wants, ya can stay in 'ere," The door swung open to reveal a small room with a couch and a desk. No windows and a tower of boxes took up one entire corner but to me it was perfect.

"Absolutely, that would be great, thank you," The enthusiasm in my voice seemed to startle him, a frown quickly passing across his face before it settled back into disinterest.

"Drop ya stuff in there and then find Shelly, she'll grab ya a uniform and show ya where everything is. You'll get food on shift and if there's food left over when you're not on shift ya can have that too," I nodded and flashed him another smile which seemed to prompt him into movement. He stomped back off down the hall and left me standing in the doorway, finally able to breathe a sigh of relief. I dropped my backpack in the room and pulled the door shut before tracking the waitress, Shelly, down. She threw a uniform at me, the fabric faded and soft under my fingertips, before shuttling me around the diner, giving me the quickest training I'd ever had.

"I'm here until midnight today, so you can work with me today, but then you'll be on your own tomorrow," she sent me a glance that was almost apologetic, but I shrugged. I'd worked by myself at every diner I'd been at in the last two and a half years, it wasn't anything new. That was why I picked the run-down diners in tiny towns. Less people to be affected by whatever trouble decided to follow me around. But Shelly didn't need to know that. A couple of people came through the door, effectively halting the conversation, so I hurried to put the uniform on as Shelly sat them down before hurrying back to shadow her.

The evening passed quickly, even though the diner was quiet and, luckily for me, there were no incidents. Even the food, though greasy, was good and the portions were huge so there was little chance of me going hungry. For the first time, part of me wished I could stay here for longer than a couple of months. As I collapsed onto the couch in the early hours of the morning, I let myself imagine for just a moment building a life in Devil's Creek, even if it was nothing but a fantasy.

The next few weeks seemed to speed by; working in the diner was easy work and Todd, the chef and owner, paid better than I expected. He didn't say much but he seemed to slowly warm up to my presence, sometimes going so far as to start a conversation with me in the mornings. Between him and Shelly, I almost felt like I was making some friends for the first time. In most of the other towns, no one had tried to talk to me. The night before my 21st birthday was the busiest day of the week, Friday night. Even the Devil's Creek Diner had somewhat of a rush on Fridays, the townspeople filling every restaurant around, ours included. In the middle of the rush, I brushed past Shelly and she grabbed my sleeve.

"I've just sat another table in your section, table 23. Just… be careful with them. They can be handsy. If they cause you any trouble just let Todd know and he'll sort them," I nodded before hurrying to drop the food off at one of my other tables before turning around to table 23. I knew before I even laid eyes on them that it was going to be the idiots in the truck.

Sure enough, there they were, leering at me from across the room. I doubted they remembered me from that one night weeks ago which meant they acted like this with everyone. Pasting on a smile, I hurried over.

"Welcome to the Devil's Creek Diner, what can I get you?" I stayed a couple of feet back from the table, hoping to avoid grabbing hands and glanced around at each of them, waiting for an answer.

"Hopefully you're on the table," one of them answered, his eyes flicking up and down my body. The guy next to him broke in with a guffaw.

"No, hopefully she's under the table sucking my d-" A shudder of revulsion broke over my back as I forced the smile to remain on my face and interrupted before he could finish his sentence.

"Can I start you off with some drinks?" A flicker of annoyance crossed over the face of the guy making the lewd comment at the interruption but he quickly recovered, shooting me a grin and licking his lips.

"Chocolate milkshakes, with *lots* of whipped cream and a cherry on top," Somehow, he even made that sound creepy, the rest of the group breaking into sniggers as I spun on my heel and stalked over to the bar. I wanted to take my time making the drinks, to stay as far away from that table as I could, but there were so many other people still needing their orders that I knew I couldn't. I threw the drinks together, topped high with towers of whipped cream and hurried back over, hoping I'd be able to drop them off and take their food orders without any more comments. They cheered as they saw me, one of them wolf whistling so loud some of the tables around them turned to stare. I felt colour flame in my cheeks and wondered if Todd would fire me for throwing the milkshakes in their faces.

This is the best gig you've had so far. Don't throw it away over some entitled jerks.

"Here are your chocolate milkshakes, can I get you any food?" I tucked the tray under my arm, pulled out the pad and pen from my apron and raised an eyebrow at them.

"Why don't you just put your ass on a plate and give us that?" the third guy, one I didn't remember seeing in the truck before, chimed in. My hand twitched, wanting to grab the nearest milkshake so badly as they all jeered and laughed. Thundering footsteps behind me, quickly followed by a huge shadow told me Todd had heard enough to make an appearance. They all quietened down as he towered over me; I didn't even need to look to know his trademark frown was in full force right now.

"She asked ya a question," he growled. The jerks at least had the sense to shrink back before hurriedly stammering out food orders. Todd stayed behind me the whole time and walked back to the kitchen with me when they were done. I caught the looks on their faces as we left and knew that I hadn't seen the end of that particular issue. Todd grabbed the food ticket off me as we got to the hatch and disappeared through the swinging doors, shooting me his attempt at a smile as he did. "If they give ya any more trouble, just give me a nod and I'll kick 'em out,"

"Will do," I flashed an answering smile and hurried off to see to the rest of my tables, keeping one eye on table 23 as I did. All too soon, Todd was calling out their number and I was on my way back over, tray laden down with food. I hoped Todd had spat in it. The guys were talking quietly amongst themselves as I approached but when they saw me, they straightened up and flashed me matching grins that made my teeth clench. "Here's your food. Two burgers," I put one each in front of the two closest to me, "and a grilled cheese," That was for the guy at the back of the booth, meaning I had to lean across the table. As I did, stretching to put the plate down since he made no move to take it from me, I felt the hand of the guy closest to me settle on my back. I stiffened, throwing the grilled cheese down with a clatter and straightened up, turning to face the one closest to me.

"Take your hand off of me," I muttered, hoping that no one else had seen him. In response, his hand dropped down to my backside and squeezed while he laughed, his friends grinning. Rage bubbled up inside my chest and before I even processed what I was doing, I had shoved him back into the seat, grabbing his arm and wrenching it off me. "Get your hand off of me!" I yelled, causing the rest of the diner to fall silent. Even the jerks seemed taken aback, the grins falling from their faces. My face flamed as I grabbed the tray and spun around, storming back to the kitchen where Todd was already on his way out.

"What happened?" he ground out, eyes already fixed on table 23.

"One of them decided to grab my ass and wouldn't let go," I could feel tears of embarrassment threatening to fall down my cheeks and I didn't want to cry in front of the whole diner. With a sob I pushed past Todd who was storming over to their table and hid in the back for a few minutes. I could hear Todd yelling, even through the doors and knew those guys wouldn't be staying for their food. Wiping a couple of tears away, I pushed back through the doors just in time to see them slinking out of the diner. They saw me as I emerged and the look on their faces sent chills down my spine, each one red with embarrassment and glaring at me with all their might. As they left, the rest of the diner slowly picked up again and Todd gave me a nod before heading back to the kitchen. I took a deep breath, heading back to another one of my tables, trying desperately to put their faces as they left out of my mind.

What a way to spend my last night as a 20 year old…

Luckily, the rest of the night passed without incident. The next day I woke to the smell of food drifting through the doors, immediately thinking I'd overslept. I jumped off of the couch and hurried out into the diner, pulling a uniform on, only to be met by an empty room except for Todd and Shelly. They both smiled at me as I emerged and stepped apart to reveal a hastily thrown together, lopsided birthday cake.

"How…" my eyes filled with tears again. I hadn't had a birthday cake since I'd left home.

"You think I don't know the birthdays of my staff members?" Todd grunted, "Happy Birthday kid," Shelly chimed in with her own happy birthday. "You've got 'bout half an hour before we open so ya might as well have some cake for breakfast," I laughed and sat down at the table, grabbing a fork and motioning for both of them to join me. I felt the most at home here, in this diner in Devil's Creek, than I ever had, even in my own home. I felt like I belonged with these people, in this town. As we chatted and stuffed our faces with cake, a telltale tingle trickled up my spine.

No. Not today.

I waited for something to spontaneously explode but everything stayed as it was, both Todd and Shelly digging into the cake. After a few minutes, I let myself relax again, but it continued to niggle at the back of my mind. The day itself passed quickly, the standard crowd coming in for breakfast and lunch, the dinner shift a bit busier than normal but nothing we couldn't handle. And, despite the tingle, there were no *incidents.* No fires, nothing breaking, not even a glass dropping. By the time the dinner shift finished, I'd almost forgotten about the tingle. Maybe I could stay here.

My last task of the night, before I could sink into the couch and sleep, was taking the trash out. I dragged the two heaving rubbish bags behind me as I shouldered open the back door to the bins. The night air was still, the moon shining down between the buildings, providing more light than the pitiful light Todd had installed over the back door. It was chilly, October in full swing now, but I loved this time of year. The trees had come alive in brilliant reds, rusts and burnished yellows, some of those leaves decorating the floor as I pulled the trash behind me. I heaved open the lid to the skip, tossing in one bag and then the other before slamming it shut and turning to go. As I did, a hand covered my mouth, another grabbing around my waist, pulling me back behind the bins to where the light of the moon didn't even dare go.

"Mmph!" I tried to scream around the hand but it was forced into my jaw even harder, threatening to crack teeth. The arm around my waist tightened as well with bruising force, fingers digging into the soft skin of my stomach. I could hear at least three people breathing around me, the two who weren't holding me blending into the darkness. Another tingle worked its way up my spine as my eyes finally adjusted to the darkness and I stared into the faces of the jerks from table 23. Their grins seemed demonic under the splintered moonlight as they moved closer and panic shot through me. I couldn't scream but I could *bite.* I opened my mouth and sunk my teeth into the palm over my mouth, biting down until I tasted blood. The one holding me let go of my mouth with a yell.

"You bitch!" I spat his blood onto the floor as he inspected the wound and I struggled again, trying to get free but his arm was like steel. The grins had dropped from the faces of the two in front of me and they forced me back against the wall by the bins.

"You're going to get what's coming to you, you little bitch," one of them whispered, his damp mouth close enough to my ear that I felt his clammy breath across my skin. "Someone like you should be begging for our attention, especially when you look like that," he motioned to my uniform, the dress hugging my body. "But instead, you got your boss to kick *us* out. Do you know how embarrassing that was for us? So we decided you needed to learn your lesson. Be *grateful* that you have our attention. Be a good little girl and get on your knees," More tears threatened to spill, misting over my vision as hands on my shoulders tried to force me to the ground. When I resisted, one of them closed a palm around my throat and squeezed, black spots appearing at the edge of my vision.

I don't think I'm going to be lucky this time…

As the world wavered in front of me, slowly drifting to black while his hand tightened, a flash of white launched across my eyes. A growl reverberated through my ears and the hand on my throat disappeared, replaced with the panicked screams of all three of the men. I slumped down the wall, fighting unconsciousness, my eyes straining to focus. All I could make out was the flash of white darting around and the sounds of tearing flesh and frenzied screaming before the world around me faded to black.

I woke to something wet on my face. My eyes fluttered as consciousness seemed to dump itself upon me in one fell swoop. Everything hurt, my throat most of all, but something was consistently dripping on my face. Finally, I managed to get my eyes open and my vision slowly came into focus even as I had no idea what I was looking at. White fur seemed to have replaced the sky above me, the dripping falling from what appeared to be an open mouth filled with sharp canines. As I shifted, trying to move back while my brain processed, the fur shifted and I came face to face with amber eyes, a long snout and a face full of smelly breath. I scrambled up, my back sliding up the wall as I took in the full size of the creature in front of me. It looked almost like a white wolf, ears pricked as it stared at me, but it was huge, at least three times the size of an actual wolf. Its body was blocking me from seeing most of the alley around us, standing over me where I sat, the cold concrete slowly seeping through my jeans. Around it's huge paws, I could see a puddle of something red and an arm and when I looked back at the wolf-creature, I saw the fur around its mouth was stained red as well. It regarded me almost thoughtfully, head cocked to one side, and everything about it seemed friendly. Cautiously, I reached a hand out, something in me wanting to sink my hands into the thick fur that covered it's body. As I was seconds away from seeing if it was as soft as it looked, the back door of the diner swung open again and the creature's head whipped around, a rumbling growl filling the air. I snatched my hand back as its fur seemed to set alight, bright white and blue flames licking across its body and shattering the darkness of the night air and it leapt forward, placing itself squarely in front of me as a shadow came out of the door.

Todd.

I opened my mouth to scream, to try and warn him but my bruised throat couldn't make a sound. The creature ran forward, flames leaving a trail through the dark. Todd stepped out into the alley, taking in the creature with a bored expression, before flicking his eyes around until he settled on me, cowering by one of the bins. The creature was almost upon him, growling and snarling as it prepared to jump and I closed my eyes, not wanting to see Todd ripped apart. A command rang out across the alley, a word I didn't understand and then the screams I expected didn't come. Cautiously, my eyes opened to see the creature sat in front of Todd, no longer alight, as Todd held up a palm that was *on fire.*

What the hell is happening?!

As if he heard me, the creature turned around and came back to me, giving me a quick sniff before sitting next to me. My hand reached out and sunk into the soft fur, the heat coming off of the creature instantly warming me through. Todd glanced left and right before picking his way across the alley; now I wasn't blocked by a wall of fluff, I could see the various piles of blood and multiple bodies ripped to pieces around me. I knew without seeing their faces that it was the men who had tried to assault me and I couldn't find it in myself to even feel slightly bad about their bloody demise. Todd similarly didn't seem perturbed, skirting the blood and bodies with a sneer of disgust but little else. Once he reached me, he held a hand out and I took it automatically, my mind still scrambling, trying to make sense of everything that had just happened.

"I think we've got a bit of explainin' to do, kid. Come on," He pulled me to my feet, the creature immediately getting up and leaning into my legs as we made our way back into the diner. The silence seemed louder than ever, the halogen lights flickering as Todd led me to a booth and gently pushed me down before sitting across from me, somehow managing to slide his huge form onto the worn leather seat. The creature sat next to me and I found my hand going back to its fur, winding deeper and twisting strands beneath my fingers.

"So," I croaked, surprised by the flash of fire I saw in Todd's eyes as he looked at my bruised throat. "What the hell is happening?" It hurt to even say a few words, but I needed answers.

"I'll be honest kid, I didn't expect it to happen like this…" he trailed off, gesturing to my bruised body and the creature next to me. I stared at him, waiting for more information and in a very uncharacteristic move, Todd sighed and swept a hand across his face. "Okay, um. I guess I'll start with him," he nodded to the creature. "That is a hellhound-"

"A WHAT?" I whisper-screeched, my hand pausing in it's fur. Strangely, I still didn't feel any panic. Nothing about the creature, despite the display I'd seen outside, seemed to be a threat to me.

"Ya gonna have to let me get through everythin' kid or this is gonna take forever," Todd snarked, "That's a hellhound. Yes, from Hell." He answered the question before I even managed to open my mouth, "He's here to protect you; in fact, he's being doin' it his whole life, you just couldn't see him," I glanced down at the hellhound and he grinned up at me, tongue lolling out the side of his mouth.

"I- I think I did see him, when I was a lot younger," I ground out and Todd blinked at me before continuing.

"I suppose that's not unheard of. You can only see him now because you've reached your 21st birthday and the glamour that prevented you from seeing him, or anything else to do with Hell, has been lifted as was agree- I'm gettin' ahead of myself. Hellhounds are a bit different from the ones we see in films. They're not all skeletal, constantly on fire, angry dogs. They mostly look like him and they can call Hellfire but they're not constantly aflame. And, as you can see, they're not aggressive unless it's needed. Hellhounds are assigned to protect demons, often demons who have been sent to Earth as children and will stay with them, preventing all disasters to that demon. Demons attract trouble, especially on Earth."

Demons? Hellhounds? Wait… they're assigned to demons-

"What do you mean, they're assigned to protect demons?" my voice shook as I asked the question, not wanting to hear the answer.

"You're not human. Neither am I. You're a demon who was placed here at birth, a changeling of sorts, with human parents to hide you until you come of age. It wasn't safe for you down there when you were vulnerable. Now, you'll come into your full powers and will be able to protect yourself. Or you will once you're back in Hell," My brain splintered, so many questions piling on top of each other. Next to me, the hellhound whined and licked my hand.

"Say I believe you – which I'm still struggling to do – why wasn't it safe for me? Why not have a demon like you look after me instead of humans? Trouble did follow me, to the point where I left to protect my, well the people I thought were my parents. Surely if another demon looked after me, you could have explained all this a lot earlier and I wouldn't have spent my life wondering why I attracted trouble like a magnet!"

"Demons like me, ones who have our full powers already, have to stay near a Hellgate, both to stop certain other demons coming out and to avoid us withering away and dying. If you were placed near a Hellgate, demons would have come through trying to find you. You had to be far enough away that no one could find you. It wasn't safe for you because a lot of demons wanted to kill you while you were vulnerable and end Lucifers reign…"

"Lucifer…?"

"You're Lucifer, the King of Hell's, daughter… Look, you'll have time to learn all of this when you're back in Hell. You'll slowly regain knowledge you had when you were born, knowledge that's been locked away this whole time. But, first, we have to do something else. Thanks to Fluffy there, you've got some clean-up to do," he gestured to the hellhound.

Fluffy? I like that!

The voice floated into my mind, definitely not my own and I jumped, glancing down at the hellhound next to me. He grinned up at me, panting.

Great. Now I'm hearing a hellhound in my MIND.

Shoving that nugget of information aside for a moment, I looked back at Todd.

"What kind of clean-up?"

"Those men that your hellhound disposed of, their souls need to go to Hell and be judged for their crimes against you. Because they were killed on your behalf, you need to take them to Hell and because you're Lucifer's daughter, you'll be deciding their sentence…" Todd trailed off as a grin split my face, the first one since I'd regained consciousness. Something dark and vengeful was taking root in my chest, burning through my veins like Hellfire.

"I get to decide their punishment?" my voice was lower, tinged with glee that I hadn't ever heard from myself before. I *wanted* to make them pay. Todd nodded and slid out of the booth, gesturing for me to follow him. Fluffy and I walked in step behind his huge form as he went back through the kitchen, down the hallway to the door at the very end that I'd never been in. Every step we took towards it seemed to unlock a part of me I hadn't known, unfurling in my chest, a part of me that couldn't wait to make them pay. Todd stopped at the door and glanced back at me.

"Brace yourself," he muttered before pushing the door open. The heat hit me immediately, flames rushing out of the doorway to meet us. They didn't burn, instead they wrapped around my body like a hug, settling into my bones like a part of me I'd been missing. "Welcome to Hell," Todd motioned me through and as I crossed the threshold, it was as though the last bits of me that had been cultivated by living on Earth fell away, leaving behind rage and vengeance. Three figures moved in my peripheral and I snapped my gaze to them, a slow grin spreading across my face as I took in my attackers. They weren't smirking now, their souls surrounded by Hellfire, fear etched into every fibre of their being.

Oh, I was going to enjoy this.

With a chuckle, I walked towards them, the Hellfire parting where I stepped, until I was just a few feet away, Fluffy by my side with his fur alight.

"Hello, boys," They shivered as I addressed them and I felt my grin stretching even further. "I've heard that I get to decide your punishment. I bet you're regretting assaulting me right now… So, I've decided you need to learn a lesson. Be *grateful* that you have my attention. Be *good little boys* and get on your knees…" Strands of Hellfire whipped out and wrapped around their throats, squeezing until their eyes bulged, forcing them onto their knees in front of me. "I hope it was worth it because now you get to experience everything you did and were going to do to me, for all eternity…" More Hellfire surrounded them and their screams filled the Hellscape.

I guess I am lucky after all…

Afterword

Hellhounds are found in mythology across the globe, appearing as guardians or gatekeepers of Hell; they are often described as large, with red eyes and black fur/skin and sometimes appear with multiple heads, such as Cerberus from Greek mythology. Sometimes, they can be alluded to as servants of Lucifer or Hades, particularly in popular culture and films.

The

Hotel

Trigger Warnings

Drugging someone against their will, murder, suffocation, implication of mass murder, discussion of dead bodies

The Hotel

History repeats itself,

as the saying goes,

patterns falling into place like puzzle pieces,

the same few on top

and the victims trampled into nothing

between the pages of the history books

We're creatures of habit after all,

only interested in the rise before the fall,

the victory painted in perfect focus

while the failings, the faults, the fissures

splinter and crack and suck in those who got too close

and it's never their fault, the innocent bystanders,

felled by villains who repeat the cycle like clockwork.

Often, we only see the pattern once it's already happened,

already absorbed into the past, the ink dry and steeped in
pain,

retroactive action to make up for sins that should have never been committed;

we see it, time and time again, but it continues

because those on the top don't care to change

and those below can't make waves,

the ruling echelons of society held up by marble pillars,

splattered with the blood of crimes they pretend not to commit.

But enough waves can topple a pillar,

buoyed by voices of victims not willing to repeat history,

not willing to sit back and let the play continue on the World's stage,

patterns disrupted by nothing more than a missing puzzle piece,

it feels tiny, inconsequential, a bug bite in the neck of society,

yet, without it, the pattern cannot complete, cannot repeat,

cannot continue to reward those with something to gain

from everyone else's pain.

History repeats itself

until the book is turned on its head

revealing the wolf in sheep's clothes,

their sins painted in scarlet on their chest,

so that, soon, no one gets left behind

between the pages of the history books.

Stranded in the middle of London on Halloween wasn't exactly how I envisioned my night going. Granted I hadn't exactly had an amazing night planned anyway; I'd wanted to be in bed by now, watching some crappy Halloween movie and eating a buttload of leftover Halloween candy. But the trains in London run smoothly for no one so here I was, shivering and alone on some random street after the last train home was cancelled with absolutely no clue what my next move was.

I knew, when my manager called me and asked if I could cover our latest event in London at the last minute that I should have said no. But she dangled a bonus in front of me and I relented with only the briefest hesitation.

Idiot.

Current Me was not impressed with Past Me's decision-making skills. I didn't imagine Future Me would be too thrilled either. A car sped past, sending me stumbling back from the edge of the road. Besides the occasional car, the road I was on was silent, full of closed businesses and high-rise buildings. I didn't even know how I'd ended up here; my phone had died along with the last bit of my hope when my train had been cancelled and I'd been wandering blindly since then, hoping for an open fast-food joint or a hotel that still had a room. It was unlikely on Halloween, but my only other option was to wander the streets all night and despite how quiet they were now, I had enough self-preservation to know that no good came from a woman being alone, at night, in London. Shaking off the shiver that accompanied that thought, I forced myself to continue walking down the street, telling myself that something helpful would be around the next corner.

More high-rise buildings.

Not quite the saving grace I'd been hoping for. With a sigh, I trudged further, eyeing the grey clouds lit only by the light of the moon and the occasional flickering streetlight. It would be just my luck if it decided to tip it down. I'd be soaked through in seconds, wearing the stupid Halloween costume my manager had sent me to the event with which seemed to be made of virtually no fabric, and the fabric that was there was so thin it might as well have been see-through. I turned another corner and my breath hitched at the building in the distance; there were lights on, which was better than anything else I'd seen so far. Feet moving with renewed enthusiasm, I hurried down the street, almost sobbing when I realised it was a hotel, the name illuminated on the side of the building.

The Marley

I'd never heard of it, but I didn't care. There were lights on, people inside and maybe even somewhere I could charge my phone, so it was basically The Savoy in my eyes. I leapt up the steps and shouldered open the gold rimmed glass door, basically falling into the lobby. Luckily, there were only a couple of staff around to witness my entrance and they seemed more horrified by my outfit than anything else. As I straightened up, I took in the lobby and immediately understood why my outfit was drawing all the wrong kind of attention. Huge chandeliers hung from the ornate ceiling, the gold glinting under the glow of what had to be hundreds of lights. The floor looked like polished marble, with huge decorative rugs swallowing up large areas, accompanied by plush velvet chairs. Everything screamed *old money*. The hotel itself looked like it had been around since the 1920's, if the bar in the corner gilded in art deco style was anything to go by. Pulling down my barely-there skirt, I located the reception desk, where my eyes met the scandalized gaze of the receptionist.

I thought this night couldn't get any worse but yet, here I am.

I fixed a polite smile on my face and hurried over, pretending I didn't see the receptionist recoil slightly as I approached. He grimaced in response to my smile but reluctantly welcomed me all the same.

"Welcome to The Marley. How can I help you?" I knew he wanted nothing to do with me but I was out of options. And starting to get a little offended. The Halloween costume might have been on the side of scandalous (and I couldn't wait to *thank* my manager for that on Monday) but it was *Halloween.* Surely, they expected people to be in costume?

"Hi. I'm sorry to come in so late, in this state, but I was hoping you had a room available? I've had a terrible night and I really just want to go to sleep…" I trailed off, sending a quick prayer to any god that was listening that there would be a room here. Hell, I'd even sleep in one of the velvet chairs at this point.

The receptionist gave me a tight smile, his fingers flying over the keyboard. "I'll have a look for you, *ma'am* but as it is Halloween, we are quite busy," We stood in awkward silence for a few moments as he continued typing, the sound seeming to echo in the quiet lobby. Each second that ticked by solidified the knot growing in my stomach. I was going to have to go back out onto the street and find another hotel, somehow. Back into the cold and probably the rain. Suppressing a shudder, I looked back up at the receptionist, his cold expression fixed on the screen in front of him. Finally, he looked up, another attempt at a smile flashing briefly across his face.

"It looks like we have one room available. But I have to let you know, it's in need of some updating, it's one of the last rooms waiting for refurbishment so there may be some cosmetic wear and tear-"

"I don't care about that, I'll take it," I interrupted, the thought of any kind of room, no matter how much 'cosmetic wear and tear' filling me with enthusiasm I hadn't felt in hours. I pulled my wallet out of my tiny bag, grabbing my credit card and placing it on the desk. "Use this card," The receptionist regarded me for a few more seconds before sighing and taking the card and sliding across a form and a pen.

"We need a few details from you, if you can fill out the form and sign at the bottom. The rate for the night is £130 and we will also hold a £50 security deposit which you will get back after check-out," he reeled off, already processing the payment. £130 had never sounded so good. I turned my attention to the form and filled it out quickly, noting the check-out time before sliding it back across. He gingerly grabbed the paper and typed a few more details in before handing back my card and a receipt. "I'll get the key for you now. You're going to be on the 9th floor, room 937. There are lifts just behind you down that corridor," he motioned behind me, "and when you get to the 9th floor just follow the signs to 937," I nodded, fingers itching to grab the key he was putting in a paper wallet. The few seconds it took seemed excruciating but *finally* he handed the key over and I all but ran to the corridor he'd mentioned.

The grandeur of the lobby continued to the corridor and just beyond I could see further into the art deco bar, filled with more plush velvet chairs and sofas and high-top tables shining under the chandeliers. Any other day and I'd be there right now, drowning my sorrows, but I wanted nothing more than to get this outfit off and into bed.

Shit. I have no clothes.

I glanced back down at the costume and grimaced.

Guess I'm sleeping in this. That's going to be fun tomorrow morning.

I couldn't wait for the looks I was going to get on the train back tomorrow morning. But that was a problem I would deal with when it arose. The lift to my right dinged, doors sliding open, and I hustled inside. It was small and didn't reflect the shiny richness the rest of the hotel had. Instead, it looked like it wouldn't be amiss in a grungy car park, half the buttons without numbers and the mirrors surrounding the lift smudged and covered in *something* I didn't want to think too much about. Even worse, the entire thing creaked as it moved, shuddering as though there was a small elephant in here. I gripped the bar, hoping the cables didn't snap and just really round off this night from Hell. Finally, we jolted to a stop at the 9th floor, the lift doors slowly screeching open to reveal a hallway that looked *nothing* like the lobby downstairs. I hopped out, noting the old, stained carpet beneath my feet, as the lift doors closed; part of me wanted to hop back in and take my chances on the streets.

The lights overhead flickered, the too bright white light strobing down the hallway. It seemed to extend forever in both directions; luckily, a worn sign on the wall pointed me to the right. With one last glance at the lifts, I set off down the hallway, the carpet beneath my feet somehow becoming worse the further I ventured. Patches of darkness interspersed with the flickering lights and the walls, covered in some very tired wallpaper, seemed to close in. In some attempt to decorate the descent into Hell, there were paintings lining the walls but each and every one seemed to be straight out of some kind of horror film. Watercolours of Victorian children interspersed with drab, macabre flowers, battle scenes surrounded by chipped gold frames. I picked up the pace, not wanting to be in this hallway for much longer in case these damn paintings came to life. Suddenly, the quiet hallway came to life with the sound of howling, sending me stumbling into one of the walls. My heartbeat furiously for a moment before I realised it was just the wind howling and not a pack of Hellhounds on their way to drag me down to my eternal punishment. The wind seemed to be *in* the hallway, so loud as it bounced off of the walls relentlessly even though I hadn't seen a single window so far.

Eventually, as the end of the corridor came into sight, so did room 937. It was the very last room in the hallway and, of course, the light above the door seemed just as temperamental as the rest of them, flickering menacingly at me when I dared approach. Hands shaking, I grabbed the keycard and slid it into the slot before pulling it back out, my other hand already on the handle, ready to get out of this hallway. But the light turned red, blinking at me like a demon eye. I tried again, another red light. The thought of walking back down the hallway, getting back in that lift and facing the surly receptionist again filled me with dread. Panicking, I looked at the card and the wallet, checking I had the right room. 937 stared back at me in neat handwriting.

Desperate, I flipped the card round and tried it the other way and huffed a sigh of relief when the light flashed green. The door flung open as I hurried to get out of the hallway, creaking as it did so, joining the chorus the wind had already created. It swung shut behind me, the heavy wood clunking back into place, leaving me in darkness. My hands felt around on the wall near the door, scrabbling for any kind of light switch; eventually I located it and flicked both of the switches on. For a second, nothing happened, then the whole room groaned as if protesting the effort and the lights flickered on. The relief in my chest was short-lived.

Cosmetic wear-and-tear my ass!

The room in front of me looked like it hadn't been touched since the 1920s. Literally. Great chunks of wallpaper had been peeled away, revealing the stained wall underneath and the areas the wallpaper remained weren't much better. To begin with, I thought the entire wallpaper was stained but it turned out that whoever did the interior design had gone with a wallpaper in shades of beige and pale pink that looked as though someone had tipped tea all over every inch of it. It reminded me of the school project I'd done in history, when we used tea bags to stain the paper to make it look 'old'. This wallpaper managed what I couldn't in my project; everything looked tired, old and miserable. The carpet was, for some reason, purple, but even that strange colour choice couldn't hide the multitude of *actual* stains that decorated it. My feet were aching but there was no way I was taking my shoes off tonight. Tentatively, I put my bag on the tired wooden vanity and crept further into the room, half expecting something to fall down on me as I moved. The curtains took up one entire wall, dark and patterned, another bold design choice by whoever had decorated. I was coming to the conclusion that they must have been blind. I didn't want to touch them, but the room felt so small and close with them shut so I shuffled around the bed and pulled the curtains open. As if it had been waiting for an invitation, the wind started up again and a rattling made me jump. On closer inspection, it seemed that one of the windows was loose in its frame and was *literally held in by a screw.*

Oh great. So, if I can't hack it in this dump of a room, I'll just push the window out of its frame and jump.

The rattling of the window continued as I turned away and I could already tell that would be annoying me for the rest of the night. But, as I surveyed the last bit of the room, the bed, I knew I wouldn't be getting much sleep anyway. The sheets themselves were stark white, a weird contrast to everything else in the room that seemed to be beige or stained, and were covered in a comforter that matched the carpet, stains and all. The frame looked older than me, the wood chipped and faded, and I was sure if I sat on the bed it would creak like a ship at sea in a storm. But it was the walls above the bed that had my attention. Surrounding the bed were three paintings, just as creepy as the ones in the hallway outside. One was another Victorian child painting, which seemed to be a favourite in this hotel, one was a dismal bunch of flowers and the third was a woman, reclining on a chaise, her eyes fixed on something in the distance. Every single one of them gave me the creeps and every single one of them was *wonky.*

Out of everything, I think the fact they're wonky annoys me the most.

I already felt like the eyes in the paintings were following me and the shiver that crawled up my spine did nothing to quell that fear.

The sooner you get to sleep, the sooner it will be morning and you can get the hell out of here.

Morning could not come fast enough. I hustled over to the bathroom, bracing myself for whatever horrors awaited in there but besides the flickering light, it was probably the cleanest and most modern part of the entire room. Even the shower curtain, when I peeked behind it, didn't hide any monsters or, even worse, spiders. Luckily for me, and my teeth, there was an amenity kit on the counter, complete with toothbrush, toothpaste, soap, shampoo, conditioner and body wash. At least I'd be clean, even if the room didn't feel like it was. Basic hygiene complete, I reluctantly headed back into the main room, flicking the comforter off the bed and checking the pillows and mattress before resigning myself to sleeping on top of the sheets. That seemed to be the safest option and at least there was heating. I laid my head back on the pillow, sending up a quick prayer that there were not bugs waiting to pounce and stared at the beige ceiling. I could see the painting of the woman in my peripheral and I was fighting the urge to get one of the towels from the bathroom and hang it up over her.

What a great Halloween this has turned into. It's very on theme at least.

I'd be stuffing my face full of Halloween chocolate when I got home tomorrow. I think I deserved at least two bags. As I drifted off, the rattling of the window became a steady beat-

-the beat carried me across the polished marble floor, spinning around with my friends as the band continued in the corner. Around us, bodies moved in sync and voices carried across the music, laughter and off-key singing filling the room. The Marley knew how to throw a party. My dress brushed my calves as I turned, ready to spin the other way, before a pair of strong arms caught me. Surprised, I looked up into an unfamiliar face as he grinned at me.

"Can I join in?" he grinned, revealing perfect pearly white teeth and a dimple in his left cheek. My stomach fluttered and I knew my friends were giggling behind me. I nodded and he didn't hesitate, spinning me out and back in, a startled noise escaping from my red-painted lips. The music reached a crescendo, the band getting into the spirit, their excitement making us dance that much faster. My new dance partner gave me a nod and lifted me into the air, towards the glittering chandeliers and I felt like I was flying into the stars. I lifted my arms up high as we twirled, people cheering all around us, before he lowered me back down, sliding down his suit until my kitten heels touched the floor. The song finished and everyone clapped but I couldn't take my eyes off of the man in front of me, his dark, slicked back hair and brown eyes that stared into mine. Distantly, I could hear my friends wandering off in search of a drink and part of me knew I should go with them, but I couldn't look away from the handsome stranger.

"Would you like to get a drink with me?" he asked quietly, his accent slipping into my ears. American. The words were out of my mouth before my brain had chance to catch up.

"Yes, that would be splendid," I murmured and was rewarded with his mouth curving into another megawatt smile, teeth almost blinding under the sparkling lights. He led me towards the bar and ordered drinks, handing me a martini before ushering us over to one of the velvet chaise longues in the corner of the room. The band started up another song and many of the people around us rushed back to the dance floor, but the man simply regarded me as he sipped his whisky. I took a nervous sip of the martini and tried not to screw up my nose at the taste; I wasn't a big drinker so it tasted horrible, but I wanted to impress him. After another sip, I went to place it on the table, but his hand stopped me.

"Drink up, it will taste better while it's still cold," he gave me a knowing smile and I flushed, wishing my inexperience wasn't so obvious. This was the first time my friends and I had been allowed to go dancing so everything was new. I took a few more gulps, draining the glass and wincing as it burned down my throat, before setting the glass on the table. The man watched me with a smile, continuing to sip his drink before starting to talk.

"What's a good girl like you doing here?" I didn't want him to think of me as completely naïve so yet again, my mouth was answering before I could stop it.

"Oh, my friends and I are here every week. We love to come to the parties here!" my voice was breathy and the giggle I let out at the end of my sentence was far too high-pitched but my head was starting to feel a bit fuzzy so I didn't care.

"Is that right? Well, it's a shame I've never seen you here before. I must have missed you," he murmured, leaning in to fix one of my curls. "Let me get you another drink," I opened my mouth to protest but he was gone before I could. My eyes closed as I leaned back against the chaise longue and when I opened them, he was back, another drink in hand. This one didn't look like a martini and was a pretty red colour. I took it from him and took a sip, pleasantly surprised by how sweet and fruity it was. It didn't taste like alcohol at all, and I found myself draining it in a matter of minutes, the sweetness from the fruit coating my lips. The fuzziness in my head increased, the pressure closing in on my temple. He chuckled and reached out, swiping his thumb across my lip before putting it in his mouth and sucking off the excess drink.

"So sweet, just like you," he whispered, and I blushed, the red creeping up my neck and staining my cheeks. "Why don't we get out of here?" he grabbed my hand, the calloused skin of his palm sending tingles across my body. Distantly, I felt myself nodding but it was as if I wasn't in control anymore. He helped me up and led me around the bar to a corridor where I was greeted by a lift and the lift operator. He gave us both a nod and tipped his hat at the man next to me before letting us into the lift and ferrying us up, up, up. I had no idea what floor we were on, the whole world was swimming, but I followed him as he led me down an ornately decorated corridor and into the room at the end, the door closing behind us with a click.

Something in the back of my mind was protesting, telling me I shouldn't be alone with him but it felt so far away. I couldn't move, even if I wanted to, my limbs were so heavy. With gentle hands, he led me to the bed in the centre of the room and I sank into the softness, loving how it felt. He disappeared out of view as I stared at the ceiling, looking at the miniature version of the chandelier above me. I could go to sleep right here quite happily. His face appeared again, right above me and he flashed me another grin, although this one didn't seem to reach his eyes. That might have been me though, everything was distorted, his face a kaleidoscope of features that didn't seem to fit together. In my peripheral, something glinted, but my head was so heavy I couldn't get it to move to look. All I could see was him. I felt his hand trail up my body, over my breasts, until he reached the neckline of my dress.

I didn't want this.

His hand gripped the fabric, fabric I'd spent weeks convincing Mother to allow me to have made into a dress, and he yanked down, so quickly I didn't even realise at first that he'd ripped my dress entirely away, leaving me in only my undergarments on the bed.

"I-" I opened my mouth, trying to tell him I didn't want this but my throat closed. When the pressure increased, I realised it was because his hand was wrapped around it, the calloused skin pressing down on my neck.

"Shhh…" he murmured. His other hand came into view and my eyes widened as I saw that the glinting was actually a knife, sparkling above me. His grin turned feral, his eyes nothing like the ones I'd seen down in the ballroom. They looked evil. My throat moved, trying to scream, cry, make any sound but he only tightened his grip.

"Shhh, good girl. You're going to bleed so prettily when I cut you open," My heart hammered in my chest, black crowding my vision. In a split second, he moved his hand from my throat and I sucked in a deep breath, ready to scream but before I could, I felt a line of fire across my neck and suddenly breathing was a lot more difficult. The knife raised from my neck, coated in my blood and, just like he'd done with the drink of my lips, he swiped his thumb across it before sucking the blood off. The black rushed back in at the edges of my vision as the knife flashed again-

154

-I shot up in bed, gasping and clutching my throat, my heart hammering as I looked for the blood. It took me a few seconds to realise there was no blood, no slit throat, no stranger in my room. Taking a shuddering breath, I tried to calm my heart rate before I had a panic attack, but I still felt like I was in the dream. As I went to lie back down, a flicker of something caught my eye. Freezing, I closed my eyes and counted to ten, telling myself that when I opened them, there would be nothing there. I opened my eyes and came face to face with a woman, her face almost see-through in front of mine. A scream tore from my throat as I scrambled back on the bed, trying to put as much distance between us as I could.

You're still dreaming. This is a dream. Wake up!

I closed my eyes again, willing myself to wake up but when I opened them, she was still there, regarding me almost softly from the other side of the bed. My heart rate was back up, pounding in my chest like a drum and my breath was short and panicked. She didn't move, didn't speak, just stared at me, her eyes sad.

Okay. Not a dream. Or, if it is, it's a really realistic one. Just get out of here.

I slid off the bed and grabbed my shoes, keeping one eye on the woman as I pulled them on and grabbed my bag. She didn't move, her eyes following me around as I hurried across the room. It was only when I got to the door, hand on the handle, that I heard it.

"Wait, please…" I paused, hand still on the door handle. That voice was so familiar, itching at my brain like an earwig. Cautiously, I stepped back into the main part of the room so I could see her. As I moved inwards, the painting of the woman caught my eye. She looked exactly like the woman in the painting on the chaise longue. My eyes flicked between the two of them multiple times before finally settling back on her. I sunk onto the bed, as far away as possible, positive that if I didn't I would fall down. *"Thank you…"* Her voice drifted through the air again and my brain suddenly put it together. It was the voice of the woman I'd been in the dream.

"What the hell is going on?" my voice wavered even as I tried to sound confident, but I was one more shock away from crying. She moved closer to me and I tensed but didn't go anywhere, holding my breath as she came to stand well, float, in front of me. "Why did I have that dream? It was *your* voice…"

Her eyes widened slightly, one hand going to her chest, but she didn't answer for a few seconds.

"You saw that? You saw… you saw what he did?" I nodded, not trusting myself to speak, when she smiled. *"Finally…"*

"I need you to explain what is going on. Or I'm leaving," I paused, snorting, "I can't believe I'm bargaining with… whatever you are. I must be losing it…"

"You're not 'losing it', you're the first person, in all this time, that's ever been able to see what happened, to actually see me and talk to me… I used to be alive so I guess I'm a ghost. I've been trapped here for so many years and I've been trying to tell someone the whole time, to talk to anyone but no one ever sees me or hears me." She took a deep breath, not that I imagine she needed to breath, but it seemed like an unconscious movement as she worked up to whatever she needed to tell me.

"What you saw in that dream, that happened to me, decades ago. My name is… was Adaline. It was when the hotel first opened and I

came with my friends, for our first ever party. I was just eighteen. And he… he got me drunk, led me up to this room and murdered me," Her voice was stronger now, filled with rage that had simmered for decades and the lights in the rooms started to flicker, just as she did as her eyes fixed on something beyond me. I flinched and she seemed to come back to herself, the lights stopping their flickering. *"He covered it up, of course. Hid my body after he'd carved it up. I watched, from here, as he sliced me up. I was the first one but I wasn't the last. He used this room for years and I saw every single girl he killed. I heard them scream and I couldn't do anything. And then he died and no one ever knew! No one knew what he did to us, what a twisted, horrible, evil man he was. The other girls, they didn't appear like I did. Even when he died, I stayed here. I didn't know why at first but I know now. I didn't want him to get away with it, even after his death. Everyone seemed to love him, but I knew the truth,"*

"And you didn't want everyone to remember him as a good man when he was a monster," I finished softly and she looked at me, tears in her eyes.

"Exactly. I've been trying for so so long to get through to someone, anyone. Someone I could tell my story to. Someone who could make sure everyone knows what a horrible man he was. I couldn't have my death be in vain. To begin with, I tried every single night, any time there was someone in this room, but no one could see me. The most I could do was make the lights flicker. Then, after a few years, I tried to reach out, completely by coincidence, on Halloween. And it was like I felt it; I felt that I got through whatever barrier was there. But the first person ran out of here screaming before I could even get a word out. As did the next. This room became known as the 'haunted' room and people stopped staying here. I tried to show

157

people what had happened but I don't think anyone else saw what you did. And then you turned up and I felt like this might be the one; I pushed my memories across the barrier first and when you woke up clutching your throat I thought that maybe it had worked. Then you saw me... and you stayed..." her voice broke off into soft sobs and I felt the strange urge to try and comfort her. I reached a hand out but, of course, it went straight through her arm. Instead, I found myself starting to talk, to cover the sound of her sobbing.

"Halloween is supposed to be the time of year when the veil between this world and the next is the thinnest. It would make sense that you could appear to people only on Halloween; but unfortunately not many people are in the mood to stick around if they see a ghost, especially on Halloween so I'm not surprised you haven't been able to talk to anyone. Not going to lie, I almost left before I even fell asleep, this room has a really creepy vibe-" She stopped sobbing and shot me a glare and I felt colour rush to my cheeks. "Sorry..." I said sheepishly. She sniffed but shot me a watery smile.

"I'm just glad you stayed. Finally, someone can do something about it!" The tears were gone, the rage back as the lights danced again. I shot her a smile even as my stomach twisted.

"What, exactly, do you want me to do about it? If I say I saw a ghost and she told me about this serial killer from decades ago, I'll be laughed at before I finish my sentence. I want to help you but I need evidence,"

She laughed, the sound somehow sinister even in her delicate voice.

"Oh, I have evidence," she stood up suddenly and drifted over the portrait. *"He was a very conceited man, and very proud of all of the girls he killed. He didn't just keep mementos… he kept us. He got this portrait done after he killed me, probably to remember his first. It's the same outfit I was wearing that night, on the chaise, down in the bar. But it also hides an important secret; if you take it off the wall and remove the backing, you'll find a key. That key opens a hidden door, behind the bed headboard. He wanted us close, you see… In that room, he's kept each and every one of our bodies, preserved and hidden for all these years. No one really paid attention to the fact this room is a bit smaller than the one opposite. He created a hidden room, somewhere he could move the bodies once he was done with us. Easy clean-up if you don't have to leave the room. Then he could come back whenever he wanted and gloat over his 'prizes',"* she spat the words with disgust and I couldn't suppress the shudder that flooded over me. If she was correct, there was a literal room of dead bodies behind the bed I'd just been sleeping on. The meagre dinner I'd had threatened to come back up, bile staining my throat. I swallowed and forced my tongue back into gear.

"That seems like a lot of work, to build an extra room in a hotel he was staying in to hide some dead bodies," She gave me a look, eyebrow quirked, a humourless smirk on her face.

"Oh, he didn't just stay at this hotel. He owned it."

I was officially incapable of any further surprises. I felt like my heart had dropped out of my stomach so many times tonight I actually wanted to check it was still in my ribcage.

"What? The serial killer who murdered you and countless other women, *owned* The Marley?"

159

"The perfect cover. He was absolute scum and didn't deserve to live but he had thought it out. No one ever discovered his crimes because he controlled the hotel and who would think twice about a young girl going missing in London?" she muttered ruefully, *"But yes, he owned The Marley. I only found this out a few years after I died, along with his name: Thomas Marley. Anyway, quickly, get the key. I only have until sunrise before you won't be able to see or hear me anymore and I want to see this bastard get what he deserves."* She prompted, spurring me into action. As I yanked the painting off the wall, part of me did wonder if I was having a mental breakdown and was about to destroy a hotel room but something in me truly believed I was actually seeing a ghost and she was telling the truth. Either way, I was about to destroy the creepy painting and I took that as a win.

I pulled the back of the frame off, flakes of cardboard floating on the sheets after years of being hung and there, stuck to the back of the painting, was a small, gold skeleton key. Gingerly, I plucked it off of the canvas and placed the painting carefully on the bed before standing up. Adaline drifted next to me as I made my way around the bed, surveying the headboard. It looked heavy and I wasn't exactly the tallest or strongest, but I'd give it a go. Adaline motioned, indicating I should push it away from us. With the key clutched in my palm, I leant on the headboard and pushed with all my might. For a second, I thought it wasn't going to do anything, but then with a creak and a groan, the whole bed moved, wobbling across the carpet. I pushed until it wouldn't go any further and then looked at the wall. At first glance, it looked like a normal wall covered in hideous wallpaper, but Adaline motioned to a certain area and as I leant closer I could

160

see a thin seam in the wallpaper and, when I moved even closer, the tiniest imperfection in the wallpaper which looked the right size for a key. Hands trembling, I pushed the skeleton key into the wallpaper, a ribbon of shock coursing through me when it disappeared into the wallpaper with a click. Slowly, I turned the key and was rewarded with the sound of a lock turning, the creaking belaying the fact it hadn't been used in years. When the key had turned ninety degrees, I paused.

Am I really about to open a room of dead bodies? After talking to a literal ghost?

Apparently, I was.

Adaline hovered by my shoulder, so close I could feel a coldness seeping into my bones. I glanced back at her and gulped; her eyes were flaming as she stared at the door, hair swirling around her face. With one deep breath, I pushed on the door, gently at first but with more force when it didn't shift. The whole room seemed to groan, the wallpaper falling away under my hand as the hidden door juddered open, revealing the hidden room. I took a quick breath in and instantly regretted it, the musty smell of air that hadn't moved in a while mingling with something... else that I didn't want to think about all that much. I hesitated in the doorway but Adaline brushed past me, taking the cold with her and floated into the room.

After a couple of seconds, I followed her, my footsteps light and cautious as I ducked through the door. The inside of the room was dark, lit only by the light from the main bedroom but I could see an old light switch off to the side that I pressed with shaking hands. The single lightbulb above Adaline's head flickered on and I immediately wished I'd kept the room in darkness. The entire room was littered with coffins, along with what looked like a medical table and a cabinet and a stack of what looked like journals.

At least they're in coffins. I definitely would have lost my dinner if they weren't.

I'd seen everything I needed to. Hell, I'd seen more than I needed to. But Adaline was floating around the room, silent tears rolling down her ghostly face. She eventually stopped in the furthest corner of the room, next to a coffin that looked much more ornate than the others and her silent tears turned into heaving sobs. I wanted to comfort her but there was no way I was walking any further into this horror show of a hidden room so I waited awkwardly by the door until her sobs faded away and she eventually drifted back to my side.

"Is this enough evidence?" she asked as we both stared at the room. I nodded, not trusting myself not to scream the second I opened my mouth. *"His name will be in those journals, I'm sure of it. I watched him writing in them after every murder. What do we do now?"* I motioned her out of the room and pulled the door shut. I didn't need to be staring at that for any longer. Even the air in there seemed to be heavy and hard to breathe. Once it was shut, I turned to Adaline and offered a weak smile.

"Now, I call the police, somehow explain to them that I stumbled across a hidden room full of dead bodies, and let them reveal the truth on the inside," She nodded and followed me across to the old, corded phone on the vanity. The phone itself was yellow with age and I grimaced at the idea of holding it to my ear but I had no charge on my phone and I'd be damned if I was going to go down to the reception and ask to call the police.

I picked it up and was relieved to hear a dialing tone. Before I chickened out, I hit 999 and waited until someone picked up.

"999, what's your emergency?" the tinny voice at the other end seemed so loud in the silent room. Even the wind had given us a break.

"Hi… I need to report a murder… well, actually a lot of murders, at The Marley Hotel…"

***

I stood across the street from the hotel, bathed in the glow of the red and blue lights, with the rest of the 9th floor hotel occupants, most of whom were in their pajamas, muttering about what was going on. The surly receptionist had spent most of the time glaring at me, aware that, somehow, this was connected to me. They all fell silent when the police brought out the first coffin, followed by another, and another. Each one that was brought out made the silence around me heavier as everyone realised just how serious this was.

The woman on the phone hadn't believed me at first, I could tell, but she sent a police car anyway. The receptionist accompanied them to room 937 but wasn't allowed in, glaring at me from the hallway; to begin with, the police asked a lot of questions and I gave them the best answers I could without revealing the ghost that stood next to me. I'd stumbled upon the seam in the wall when trying to retrieve my phone from under the bed and, curious, I'd searched the whole room for a way in. Then I showed, rather than explained and as soon as they saw the hidden room and the coffins, they leapt into action. The age of the coffins, and the rest of the evidence in the room pointing towards Thomas Marley meant I wasn't worried about the police thinking I was involved so I didn't bother sticking around much after that. Adaline followed them into the room, watching as they opened the first coffin and nearly threw up which I took as my cue to leave. The receptionist had followed me back down to the lobby, peppering me with questions but I refused to tell him anything and soon enough, more police arrived, along with forensic scientists, and began evacuating the 9th floor of the hotel. They loaded each coffin into a van, probably to take them for forensic examination, and the sheer amount of them still had nausea churning in my gut, even after seeing the hidden room. Finally, they carried out the last one, the most ornate and my stomach clenched, knowing it was Adaline. Seconds later, I saw her ghost following it out, floating out of the hotel for the first time in decades. She watched as it was loaded into the van and the doors were shut before looking up and across the street, her gaze finding mine.

I smiled and she smiled back, even as her eyes were sad. As the first rays of sun broke over the horizon, painting the street, she mouthed two words,

"Thank you…"

Then, the next ray of sun drenched the front of the hotel and her form shimmered before disappearing into the dawn, melting away as if she'd never been there. I turned and began walking down the street to the train station, more than ready to be done with this batshit crazy Halloween. Next year, I was staying home.

Afterword

Halloween, otherwise known as All Hallows Eve or Samhain is regarded as the time when the veil between our world and the Land of the Dead is the thinnest, allowing ghosts and other supernatural creatures to communicate with or even enter our world.

Ghosts, particularly those who have been killed or died in a traumatic way are often said to remain in the place they died, sometimes intent on vengeance or unable to move on until something is resolved.

Acknowledgements

By The Light Of The Harvest Moon was an idea that only came to me a couple of months ago, one I felt compelled to write and get out into the world. There wasn't much time before I wanted to release it so it turned into a huge undertaking and I couldn't have done it without the support of so many family members and friends.

First, thank you to Mum who read and edited every single one of the stories, on a very short turnaround, without any complaints; I literally couldn't have done this without you!

Dad, for continuing to support me and believe that I can do anything I put my mind to, even if it sounds crazy.

Barney, for listening to my many woes and 'I can't do this' and telling me that I could, in fact, do this. I won't say this often but, you were right.

All my friends who continue to show support for me and my writing; every time you share, like, comment or tell me how excited you are to read it, it makes me so unbelievably happy, so thank you.

Finally, to the readers, I hope you've enjoyed By The Light Of The Harvest Moon; I've put so much of myself in this collection and I'm so grateful for your support.